BILL CONVERTITO
THE ROMBELLA SHUTTLE

MAJOR BOOKS • CANOGA PARK, CALIFORNIA

MAJOR BOOKS
21335 Roscoe Boulevard
Canoga Park, California 91304

PRINTED IN THE UNITED STATES OF AMERICA

ISBN 0-89041-160-3

THE
ROMBELLA
SHUTTLE

PROLOGUE

Life in the salt mine was at last becoming tolerable.

Some of the scouts had tried existence in the world outside and they reported that the corrective surgery that they had all sustained was successful. They could now breathe comfortably in Earth's atmosphere.

There were sixty of them living in the space ship now. Soon, perhaps, some of them would go outside and begin to perform the tasks that they would be assigned.

It had taken six months of nearly dormant posture, intravenous feeding during a semi-comatose state, and a bit of surgery after the travelers aboard had become acclimatized to Earth and its atmosphere, but now they were all in good health, eager to get out of the vast spaceship that had been a prison to them for too long.

During the time of acclimatization, they were indoctrinated with all of the information available about the planet they had invaded. Alphabet, language, slang, history, customs, all had been put on tapes and fed into the minds of the people aboard the space ship. It was a painless process, accomplished without the subjects being aware of the procedures.

Olva knew that she had slept for a time. When she woke she knew everything there was to know about the world she was about to enter. Back on their home planet, the vast spaceship had been the integral nucleus of a hospital commune; sterile, the entire commune sealed against the ravages of the disease that was wiping out their population. And when it was time, the vast ship lifted up into the sky to begin the odyssey of desperation that finally brought them to a hidden sanctuary deep in a salt mine. The even temperature in the mine, the lack of humidity, too, were important to their engineers, she knew.

Olva knew that she was beautiful, even by Earth's standards. Some of those who had been in the outside world told her such things. She faced the mirror in her own private cubicle and inspected the face that looked back at her. There was immense gravity in the big gray eyes and the tendency to smile made her mouth exceptionally lovely, she thought. Her long golden hair framed an oval face and added to her beauty. People were always telling her about her beauty. She liked hearing it.

She was sixteen earth years old and, admittedly, a little nervous about the world outside.

They did not intend to remain on earth. They would stay long enough to accomplish their aims and then return home.

Her eyes filled with tears when she thought about home. It was a land very far away, a place of breathtaking beauty and heartbreaking sterility. All of the planets in their galaxy had developed a kind of progeria, a premature senility, and the people had died; all except those who had been locked away in the hospital commune.

Olva knew that William Number One was blamed for the death of her people, but he insisted that disease had been rampant before he began his experiments. And when the depopulation occurred, he hastened to the planet Earth to continue his important work.

William Number One, their gifted biologist, had finally discovered the substances that could provide the miracle her dying people had needed. But it would not work on their planet.

It worked miraculously, dependably, on earth.

William Number One had developed drugs that were aphrodisiacs, and others to shorten the gestation period to three months. He had been on earth six months now and the population explosion that was causing great agitation was phenomenon that Earth's scientists could not yet comprehend. William Number One and his helpers were still roaming the world, seeding water supplies, the atmosphere, the farms, with the irresistible aphrodisiacs, and the drug that sped gestation.

Rombella, the largest in a chain of five planets, was home to her and they would return again when it was safe to go back and their homeland would be free of the germs and the disease that decimated their ranks, at first, and then wiped them out. William Number One, when put on trial for genocide, insisted that his experiments had been intended to benefit the agriculture, and, perhaps, ideally, to increase the fertility in the peoples. Unfortunately, the drugs had destroyed the populace.

The drugs that William Number One developed reversed the life process. Instead of growing older, people regressed to the state of infancy and then died. Those who were at work in the hospital commune, the special ones, had locked themselves into the sterile precincts of the hospital and its laboratories. They had to survive. And they did survive, but it became apparent, in time, that they were all sterile.

It was decided by the Superiors, the leaders, that William Number One would be sent to the planet Earth. The inhabitants of Earth were almost identical in structure and once William Number One thought he had perfected his system of producing children in great numbers, the Superiors decided that he should go to Earth and practice his procedures there.

He and seven helpers were loaded aboard a shuttle craft and sent out into space with little or no fanfare. That had been half a year ago and now there was chaos on Earth as a sudden population glut brought new and impossible problems.

Olva laughed when she thought about it all. She knew that the babies would go to Rombella. It would begin as soon as the Wardens and the Superiors decided how and when to begin the shuttle of babies. She did not know too much about the actual evacuation procedures, but she did know that it was possible for a couple of the wardens to enter a hospital and freeze all the humans into immobility for as long as desired. The babies could be moved then,

10

sealed into one of the shuttle ships and sent off into space, guided and controlled by laser beams that would establish the trajectory and landing procedures.

Some of them would have to go back to care for the newcomers. She hoped that she would be one of them.

The elements that had caused disease on Rombella had been eradicated by William Number One and his assistants, but too late for those who had been its victims. However, it was determined that the new people would survive and prosper and breed and that was what was needed. It would require millions to populate Rombella alone, then there were the other planets in the chain, too. They would all be busy, very busy.

She was brushing her hair when the page opened her sliding door and stepped inside. It was Glota, a very pretty brunette, one of her friends.

"They want everyone in the conference room," Glota said.

Olva smiled. "All right," she said. "I'll be along."

Like all of the other females, she wore a halter and shorts and she knew that she looked very alluring. But it was all a waste. Like all of the others, she was sterile.

She stepped out of her cubicle onto the moving horizontal escalator, along with the other girls. The moving belt carried her to the doorway of the conference room and Olva stepped off. She sat in her usual chair and waited for the others to take their places.

She sensed that there was trouble.

The men in the room sat at a triangular table, ten on each side. At each point, a special chair projected outwards, the seat of a Superior.

Omborg, the Number One Superior, sat at the head of the triangle, Kaffal, Number Two, sat at his

11

left and Rissel, Number Three, sat at the right.

Each of the men and women at the table possessed exceptional skills or training in certain fields.

Olva was a medic, a surgeon, skilled in the use of the laser as a scalpel. She could perform the most delicate surgery with complete success every time.

Accidents did not happen to the people of Robella.

Except the most awful accident of all, of course. She watched the other females take their seats, impressed as usual by the beauty of the girls. For a long time, their beauty-care programs had been their only interests. She and the other females had spent most of their lives in confinement, trying to become as beautiful as possible, hoping, constantly, that they could attract a mate and produce a child. And, of course, it was all wasted effort. Still, they spent hours in the beauty shops, performing their assigned tasks in splendor and a sense of futility.

Omborg motioned in the air with his forefinger and the resonance of a gong brought everyone to immediate attention.

Omborg began to speak and the others listened with great respect.

"Our mission on this planet is in danger of failure. William Number One and those who work with him are doing their work well here. It is time for us to begin harvesting the crop of humans that we hoped for. It is time for many of them to be sent to Rombella.

"And this is where we face failure.

"Our computers do not function in Earth's atmosphere with the precise accuracy that we must achieve to guide our shuttle ships through the doorway into the proper time and space continuum."

Lichela, a gorgeous brunette Warden, spoke up.

"Does that mean that we are marooned here?"

Pillwick, a slender man of great good looks,

turned to look at Lichela. Olva was sure he liked Lichela and would mate with her if the chance presented itself. Even if it was a useless procedure. He was one of the engineers who had designed the system of computers that were buried deep within their ship.

"There are many impurities in Earth's atmosphere. The people who live here seem to have adjusted to the carbons and hydrocarbons in their air, and, presumably, we will also, but the machines cannot adjust. We will have to labor mightily to make corrections, but until we can do that, yes we are, indeed, marooned here."

Omborg spoke again.

"We shall choose three emissaries who will seek out William Number One and his helpers. They must be told to stop what they are doing, because this planet is quickly becoming glutted with infants. That was not what we intended."

Rissel, Number Three, said, "Do we care what happens to this planet?"

Omborg answered as Superior Number One should answer.

"How many planets do we want to destroy?"

Kaffal, Number Two Superior, said, "The Earth people suspect our presence here. We must hope that we can continue to remain here undetected, until we can accomplish what we must do. But, we must stop the runaway population growth. If we deplete the resources of this planet, and bring it annihilation, we, too, will be annihilated."

Omborg looked at Kaffal. He smiled.

"You seem to like the language of this world. You do well with it. And, your logic is incontrovertible. We will send the emissaries and hope that they can find William Number One and his helpers and persuade him to cease."

Olva sat, smiling, silent, watching as three tall,

handsome young men were selected to leave the ship and the salt mine. The conference was ended by Omborg and they were all excused by silent telecommunication.

A tall, handsome young man whose name was Thenna smiled at her. His thoughts came alive in her brain and no one else knew that they were talking to each other.

"I like you, Olva," he said, silently. "I would like to play a game with you after the evening meal."

She smiled at him. He was very handsome, very appealing.

"That would be nice," she answered. "I must return to my cubicle and have my dinner. Then, when it is time, I will go to the recreation rooms like everyone else. If you ask me then, I will gladly acquiesce. You are very handsome, very strong. I am pleased that you find me alluring."

He smiled. "I am one of those chosen to sabotage the computers that will betray us and our location. I leave in the morning. But, I will relish a pleasant evening with a pretty girl."

The young man made her a little bow and then left the conference room. She watched him go, wondering if they would become friends. She liked him, and she suspected that he liked her.

She was about to leave, too, when Omborg's voice intruded in her brain and she listened. Everyone else was hearing him, too.

"We will remain here while the search for William Number One is being made. There is plenty of food and we have many diversions that will keep us busy when our daily chores are done."

Kaspin, the tall, handsome chief of the wardens, spoke with great misgivings, and everyone knew it.

"We are not as safe here as we should be. While this civilization is relatively advanced, they are centuries behind us intellectually, mechanically.

Earth's computers and the interlocking data processing centers that are here now, present a great danger to us. We have intercepted some of the transmissions and the machines are beginning to suggest the possible presence of aliens as the reason for the sudden upsurge in the birthrate. And, they recommend a diligent, constant search for us. I think it is time for us to dispose of some of the computer centers. The one most dangerous to us is in Washington, the capital of the country we are in now. I intend to see to it that this complex ceases to be a danger to us."

Omborg said, "We do not wish to injure people. Remember that."

Kaspin nodded. "I shall remember. Now, we must do something about recreation. Many of our people wish to go outside into the world."

"Perhaps we will allow certain of our peoples to go out onto the planet, but we must be very selective. We must choose people with excellent judgement. For instance, what do you suppose might happen if you were talking with an earthling and you became frightened for some reason and slipped into invisibility? There would be panic among those who saw such a thing. We must avoid such situations at all cost. We must keep our presence here a secret for as long as possible. Until our present difficulties are resolved, at least.

"However, as long as we are going to be here for some time, perhaps we will try to become a part of the society around us. We will work toward that end. And, now, we all have other things to do."

It was over and they all left the conference room and the moving belts carried them back to their assigned cubicle. Olva smiled at Thenna as she went past him and her brain told him that she would see him later in the recreation room.

In her own cubicle, she glanced at the wall clock

and while she was noting the time, the feeding slot clicked and her dinner slid down into the shallow receptacle she ate from. She swallowed the capsule, drank some water from the fountain set in the wall and then disrobed, ready for the shower.

She stood for a time, admiring the sleek, virginal beauty of her body, she shook her head and the long golden hair bounced and shimmered and she sighed, wondering if she would ever be allowed to roam the planet so that people could see that she and her companions were nice looking, too.

She showered and dressed in fresh things; a pale pink halter and matching shorts. Pink slippers in the exotically shaped heels and toes. She left her cubicle, rode the moving belt to the recreation rooms and joined the people who were watching an Earth television program.

It was being screened on one of the huge scanners, the vast receiving panels that served them well during flights through space. Olva did not care much for Earth television. None of the others aboard did, either. It was always easy to predict how the dramatic shows would turn out and the variety shows were not that entertaining. But they watched because there was much yet to be learned about the things that were important to Earth people. She had no idea if her vocabulary was up to date. Always, there was much that she did not comprehend on the big screens. She was very pleased when Thenna came to her.

He smiled at her and she looked up at him, admiring him, liking him. They shared special thoughts and he took her hand and led her out of the area.

The ramps were down and some of the people were wandering about in the passageways of the salt mine. She liked the rather bright luminescence in the vast cavern. Thenna took her hand and they walked for a while.

16

She looked up at the ceiling above her head and marvelled at its undisturbed appearance. Yet, the night that they had landed, the disintegrators beneath the ship had opened up a huge crater. Then the ship came to rest inside and the overhead disintegrators reversed the process, using materials from the crater walls. Now no Earth man could tell they were here, because the outside terrain was just as it had been before they disturbed it.

Olva didn't want to think about Earth people. It was much nicer to think with Thenna, to hold his hand and walk with him in the opalescence of the enormous chamber.

She liked Thenna and she sensed that he liked her.

That was one of the things about earth people that she could not comprehend. They fell in love. A girl met a boy and they liked each other and then they went through all sorts of emotional agonies and then it all worked out all right and she wondered about it. The television screen was constantly busy with love and that was something they had on earth that she would have to learn more about.

Thenna read her mind and his smile was warm and happy.

They came to a bend in the passageway where there was a place to sit and commune.

She turned to look at him and he read her thoughts and answered her.

"We cannot go outside without permission. You know that we dare not."

He shivered slightly as he received her reply:

"If you do not want to go with me, I shall go alone. I will not stay here, cooped up in this place. I have to see what is outside."

He shook his head. "This force field will stop you."

"It does not work on us. We simply become invisible and move through the field. You know that."

"You will be punished."

She smiled. "We will be punished. You are going with me."

He stared at her, adoring her.

He sighed.

She reached for his hand and took it into her own. Slowly, they began to walk toward the distant curves of the passageway. They bumped into the force field's outer limit. A moment later they became invisible and stepped through the force field without any resistance at all.

"Let us remain this way," she said. "We can walk in complete freedom and look around."

He squeezed her hand and she could feel it even though she could not see him. He reminded her:

"I must be ready to go out in the morning with the other saboteurs. We have been ordered to cripple the computer data centers and there are others who will sabotage the infra-red cameras that their airplanes can use to locate us. We are in very real danger of being detected and we must protect ourselves."

"Of course," Olva said.

They rounded a bend in the salt mine's passageway and walked off into the darkness that was just ahead.

He squeezed her hand again and she turned to look at him and he was visible again. So was she. Smiling, they walked on through the dark pathways that led to the outside world.

CHAPTER ONE

He stood at the window and watched the sudden excitement in the parking lot. A long black limousine came to a halt close to the building's entrance. Two escort cars drew up behind it and the men in them got out first.

Martin James, head of the busy Institute of Applied Logic, a very highly developed think tank and computer data-processing center, awaited the arrival of Senator Randolph Mapes. There had been a call first and the senator had asked if he could come over and talk about the subject that was in everybody's mind.

Babies. There were just too many babies being born, they were being hatched out after astonishingly short periods of gestation, Senator Mapes, representing the U.S. government, had revealed the government's growing concern about what was taking place just about everywhere. And Martin James and his associates were just as much baffled as anyone else.

Martin James went back to his desk and sat down. A moment later, Nora Corwin walked in. She stood for a moment, smiling, showing her even white teeth.

"I would love to sit in on this."

"You don't have to, not really. You know what he wants. And we know why they've sent him. We can't say no to an old friend and the big wheels know it."

She moved closer to the desk and helped herself to a cigarette from the box in front of him. She picked up the lighter, flicked it and put it back again. She blew a streamer of smoke towards the black glass windows and then sighed. She looked at him.

"Lunch?"

"All right. I'll buzz you after the senator leaves."

She pressed a key down on his intercom panel. He started to close it again but she shook her head, pushed his hand away.

"I can listen if I want to. And I want to."

"The senator says bad words sometimes."

She made a face at him. "I say bad words, too."

Their conversation had the flavor of idiocy and they realized it. He shrugged and settled back in his chair.

The girl in the outer office buzzed him to say that the senator had arrived and was waiting for him. Nora smiled and waved. She went out and he waited until the door closed behind her to tell the receptionist to send the senator in.

He was very fond of Nora. Very fond. She was a brilliant biologist, a hard worker. She was a blonde, with large blue-green eyes. They were probably her prettiest feature. She was a pretty girl with a quick, frequent smile, a tendency toward putting weight on if she didn't exercise. Her mouth was soft and attractive, her lower lip trembled when she was upset or angry about something. She was his dear friend and a good associate.

They spent a great deal of time together and he had learned that her fine, analytical mind could be helpful. They talked most of the institute's problems out over the lunch table, at her tiny apartment, on long and companionable drives. He supposed that someone would come along and steal her from him one day and he would miss her horribly. She was irreplaceable. And adorable.

Gracie, the girl at the front desk, brought the senator into his office. They shook hands and then sat down. The glass window wall let them look out over the bustling city and its sun-tipped environs. The obelisk of the Washington Monument was in the distance, bright and shining in the sunlight.

It was early April and spring was alive and at work in the world. And, of course, there were others alive and at work in the world. And now they would have to talk about it.

Randy Mapes, U.S. Senator, head of several important committees, took out a white handkerchief. He wiped his moist face.

He looked to be very worried. And he was.

"Marty," he said, "you and your people have to help us on this. Something must be done, and quickly. The president is prepared to declare a state of national emergency, and we have the best brains in the world working on the problem."

Marty smiled at him. He leaned forward. "Why have you come to us?"

Randy Mapes became a bit testy. "You know why I've come here. You've got all of these machines, you have these damned computers around the world, all hooked in to each other and they say that you and your people and your machines can find the answer to anything. That's why I've come to you."

He was silent a moment. He sat back and looked Marty in the eye. "The president told me to come to you," he said.

The senator glanced at the intercom panel on Marty's desk.

"Hello, Nora," he said. "Why the hell don't you come in here and listen?"

Nora said, "Thank you. I will."

Marty said, "Pick up Dave on your way in."

He stood and walked over to the window wall. He looked out at the city below. It was a bright, sunny day and the dome of the Capitol building glistened with morning brilliance. It was always a reassuring sight for Marty and he liked to look at it. He loved all of the buildings in Washington, especially his own sixty-four stories of busy offices, computers and labs and libraries. He had learned that mankind always wants to know things, always wants an answer to questions and his vast complex of computers and analyzers had accomplished some remarkable feats.

With the same relaxed preoccupation the crossword puzzler exerts when resting from Einsteinian chores, they had fed the clues and details of several ancient murder cases into the complex and had actually achieved provable solutions to the previous enigmas. However, after the passage of many years there was nothing they could do about any of it. But it was fun, Marty supposed.

There were six floors devoted to medical problems and hospitals and doctors could feed symptoms and readings directly into the system and arrive at instant diagnoses, a prognosis, recommended procedures and medications to be used. The billing elements of the complex were also efficient and would even dun a subscriber if necessary.

Several of the top floors were concerned with agricultural matters and new methods of achieving the utmost productivity from the world's farms. The first recognition of a new element in the world's food supply had shown up in that area.

It had been a gradual thing. The first completely formed premature baby born to a young girl in up-state New York had been an item of curiosity. Then there were more, and more and now the world was glutted with millions of infants. The human race was propagating with the speed of rabbits. It was a very serious problem now.

Senator Randy Mapes was a big man, a handsome man, just going gray at the temples. He spent a great deal of time on television and Marty had suspected that the man was a publicity hound, until he met him. Then he discovered that Randy Mapes was one of the men who worked and did things and that was why he was newsworthy. They had become friends and Randy Mapes often stopped in for talk, but this visit, he had warned, was official.

Mapes was forty-five, perhaps, Marty supposed. Ten years older than he. The senator had it made, Marty thought. Two nice kids, a slim, lovely young wife, a beautiful estate back in his home state, a house that had been passed from father to son for many generations. That kind of background.

He stood up and Marty did, too, as Nora walked in, followed by Dave Trumbull and his pretty little wife, Lily. She was a brunette, petite, lovely, brilliant. Dave was a big man, tweedy, the crooked-pipe type, slow and methodical and brilliant in his reasonings. Dave was a psychologist and Lily was a physicist and they were constantly wrangling and arguing about the importance of each field. They were associates, dear friends, valuable assistants and Marty was now glad that they had been willing to work with him in the early days, when the Institute of Applied Logic was just an idea. He sat down again and smiled while Dave shook hands with the senator and the women sat down on one of the couches in the vast office.

"You all know why I am here," Randy Mapes said. "We have to stop the babies. We have exhausted all of our bureaucratic resources and now we must come to you. We have to hope that you and your associates and your vast complex of mechanical brains can find the answer to our problem. Something must be done. And quickly. We have hundreds of millions of babies in the world now and more on the way. We must find out how it is done."

Lily said, "We all know how it is done."

Randy Mapes turned to look at her. He had a worried, harassed look on his face. "You know what I mean. It must stop. These babies grow very quickly. They walk three days after birth. We will soon be overrun by babies."

Marty sat back in his high-backed chair. He said, "We've been working on it," he said. "Without fees, of course. We assumed that it was a national problem and we might be able to help."

"Have you learned anything yet?" The senator looked to be relieved, encouraged.

Lily said, "We have found out quite a bit, but, it is just the sort of thing that everyone else knows by now."

David had an odd little trick of taking his glasses out of his shirt pocket and putting them on before he spoke. He did it and then made a speech.

"All of the information that we have been able to glean so far suggests that extraterrestrial aliens have brought a new way of life to this planet. It is inconceivable to suppose that our agriculture has accidentally engendered a new enzyme or germ that would do such startling things. First, we must face the realities of what is taking place and realize that such things have never before happened on earth. Never."

Lily said, "The usual period of gestation has been changed in all instances that we have been able to learn about. And, the urge to reproduce is suddenly much too powerful in the human now. Therefore it must be assumed that we are being fed substances that influence human behavior as well as the reproductive processes. That suggests other world aliens to me. And to the world's best minds, too."

David went on. "The period of gestation is now three months. And these are a different kind of infant, extremely advanced even at birth. And the saturation system that is producing millions more infants than usual suggests that someone wants us to have babies.

"But why? The machines can deal with the known facts but drawing an inference is not so simple. We have been gathering data from the brain banks all over the world and the information is now being sorted and digested by the terminal computers. And we have already been offered one possibility.

"It is suggested by the machines that this planet has been invaded by aliens and they have turned this planet into a gigantic breeding farm. Perhaps their planet is dying and they need new people. But here our computers become baffled. There have been no reports of children being stolen as yet. Why not? If our theory is tenable?"

"Perhaps they have to reach a certain age in order to survive in the new environment. Could that be?"

Lily was thoughtful.

Nora said, "If we are right in our reasonings, there must be many of them alive and well and prepared to care for children. Or, are we letting our imaginations run away with us? Maybe it is an accident of nature that we are dealing with."

Randy Mapes stood up. He put his cigar out in the ash tray on Marty's desk.

"Will you take on the task of finding out what is going on, Marty?"

"Do we have a free hand?"

Randy Mapes put a big hand up to mold the flesh of his face. He was a bit more pink than usual.

"Orville Corby has been asked to look into things, too. By another department, of course. I don't trust Corby. Everyone knows that he copied your systems and set up the Association of Laboratory Logic and he has prospered."

Lily spoke up again. "He tries to steal from our machines. We have caught him at it. But, we know he is doing it so we give him lots of crazy stuff to steal."

"He does get things done, though," Randy Mapes said. "That is why one of the cabinet members asked him to see what he could come up with. A national calamity like this, we need every brain we can acquire. We must proceed toward a solution to this problem with all possible haste."

Marty said, "What about Warren P. Bowman? Do you suppose he could be responsible for any of this?"

Randy Mapes shook his head. "No. Bowman just took advantage of what has been happening. He is a lobbyist and he will always be a lobbyist, but before the boom in babies began, he decided that they should have representation and he started the Institute of Infantile Interests. Now he represents all of the manufacturers of baby products. Toys, medicines, anything and everything pertaining to infants has to be approved by his institute. He latched on to a gold mine. I think he is reasonably honest, though. And I don't think he is responsible for all the babies being born. It is going on all over the world."

"Not really," Lily said. "There are sections of the world as yet untouched. Australia, for instance, has a zero-population growth. Alaska is unaffected and the other cold continents, too. It seems to be most popular in the thickly populated regions."

Nora stood up and Marty glanced at her. She had her palms stuck into the pockets of her smock and she seemed to be unusually solemn.

"Assume that we have been invaded by aliens and that they are responsible for the boom in babies and the state of mind that we now have, and I mean the overwhelming urge to reproduce, where could such aliens hide? Can we find them? Surely they could not conceal their presence."

Randy Mapes said, "The Pentagon is pulling out all stops in that area. We have planes up at all times, crisscrossing suspect terrain. They are photographing the earth's crust with infrared cameras, hoping to expose the presence of an alien, but, so far, nothing. The people in the armed forces are using metal detectors and some really sophisticated equipment trying to locate a sunken space ship. They have announced that they are conducting maneuvers but we all know what they are really doing. But, the search will go on."

Marty stood up and Randy Mapes smiled a bit sadly.

"Money is no object," he said. "If you will send through a requisition it will be processed immediately. And, of course, you may ask for any reasonable amount."

Marty stood, looking at the senator, aware that he was with one of the finest minds in Congress.

"What do you think about all this?" he asked.

Randy Mapes hesitated. Then he said, "I just don't know. The thought of an alien presence being amongst us is fanciful, I'm afraid. I don't believe it."

"What do you believe?"

Randy Mapes smiled. "I believe it is time for you and your people to get to work on this."

He shook hands with everybody and then went out. Marty walked over to the window wall. He lit a cigarette and watched the senator get back into his car. The entourage moved out of the lot. Marty turned back to the others.

"We will have a conference at four."

David and Lily left then.

Nora lingered for a time. She sat down in the chair in front of his desk and stared at him, not seeing him, lost in thought. He flicked his cigarette lighter under her nose and held out a cigarette and she came back to him. She smiled.

"Do you honestly think that there is a possibility that we have been invaded by extraterrestrial forces? It just does not seem possible. Where was our radar? We are supposed to have a foolproof umbrella, an impenetrable cover. Oh, we can be invaded, foreign planes or mechanisms can come here but not without being detected."

He smiled, too. "We like to believe that sort of nonsense, but I don't think we can. Not any more."

Nora agreed. She went off to her desk and he sat for a time, thinking, trying to sort out the things that were in his mind. The machines were busy, sorting, analyzing, distilling information and, applying the laws of logic, were formulating presentations that would be delivered upon request. But, could they trust the fanciful suspicions that the machines were dealing with now? He wondered.

He took Nora out to lunch and they drove for a while in brilliant sunshine. His car, a nineteen twenty-seven Deusenberg in mint condition, was a thing of great beauty and he knew that Nora loved to ride in it. They listened to the radio for a while and then parked in front of a roadside restaurant just outside of the city. They went inside and ate a leisurely lunch, confining their conversation to banal, amiable badinage. There was always the possibility that they had been followed, their conversations recorded by interests inimical to their own.

The building that housed their offices and equipment was checked constantly for bugs or sophisticated spying devices, and, whenever the thin, high whistle shrilled, it exposed an area that had recently been bugged. It was a constant process. Outside people, interested in what the Institute was busy with, would send in experts to plant a bug or a device and the building's built-in snoopers would be affected by the new presence and the whistle would go off, loudest in the area where the plant was located. Probably the most vicious assaults upon the institute's privacy came from outside attempts to break the machines' codes, and, while there had been some instances of alarm, the institute usually managed to keep its secrets.

But, Marty knew, others were now working on the baby-boom problem and with varying purposes. Warren P. Bowman, head of the Triple-I, the Institute of Infantile Interests, would love to identify the source of the baby boom and then control it, exploit it. Warren was a power-mad opportunist, like many others, but there was a sort of vicious dedication to the things that he did, a complete lack of interest in the rights and privileges of those outside his milieu. He cared only about infants and their needs. He had provoked many strikes since the inception of his institute and his activities had forced prices up in the industries that dealt with the needs of infants. In spite of this, parents seemed to like him, because he made certain that baby products were safe, and that toys or items designed for babies were not made in a shoddy fashion.

Some of the magazines had done informative pieces on Warren P. Bowman and his efficient institute and they all mentioned the rapport that seemed to exist between Bowman, his institute, and the parents of America. They trusted him to make sure that everything offered to their children was safe, well made, or nourishing and palatable. Warren made the TV advertisers prove everything that they claimed. He was responsible for much that was good, but he had become overbearing, and some thought, much too powerful.

Martin had met Bowman many times and did not like him. They had argued on some of the talk shows and Bowman had said that he and his organization were planning their own vast complex of computers and analyzers, and he hoped to be allowed to subscribe to the endless informational services that Martin's concern was able to dispense with such well-publicized dependability.

Bowman was jealous, Martin supposed. And he was power mad, of course, but he just did not have the type of organization that could achieve the presently worrisome events of the recent past.

But someone was doing it. And it had to be stopped.

He sat for a time at his desk, wondering, trying to accept the things that the machines were offering as a possible explanation of what was going on and he knew that he could not accept such concepts. People from outer space, indeed!

He worked at his desk, reading reports and at five minutes before four, his secretary called and told him that he ought to hurry along to the conference.

He put the paperwork into a drawer and locked it. The pad on the wall beside the private elevator glowed as he put the palm of his right hand against the metal. The elevator door slid open and he stepped forward and then got the shock of his life. There was a beautiful blonde girl in the car. She was standing beside a handsome young man.

The golden girl smiled and he noticed that her eyes were large and singularly beautiful. She said, "Hello. I am Olva and this is Thenna."

He nodded. The elevator had not moved from his floor.

"How did you people get into this elevator? This is a private car. You will have to go back the way you came."

The girl smiled again. "No. We must do what we have come to do. Thenna is going to destroy your machines and you may watch, if you like."

The handsome young man stared at her, wondering. "Why do you tell him such things?"

"He will not remember." She raised her arm and snapped her fingers and Martin stood frozen into immobility, capable of hearing, but unable to move. The girl's smile of triumph seemed to suggest that she was testing her powers with him. He realized that she was lovelier than any young girl he had ever seen before and he wondered why he should think that way. She was blonde, average height but her complexion was flawless, there seemed to be a subtle luminescence to her skin, a light golden patina. Too, there was an exceptional luminescence in her eyes. The effect was rather startling.

The young man had the same flawless skin, the same type of brilliance in his eyes. Marty supposed that they were extraterrestrial beings and he accepted them as such. The girl was wearing pale pink shorts and a halter and the young man was wearing a pair of slacks and a T-shirt.

The girl waved her hand in the air and he was able to move again. Her smile twinkled at him and he knew that he liked the pretty invader.

"Come along with us," she said.

He had no intention of going with them and she seemed to know it. She stared into his eyes and he felt his mind disintegrating. He obeyed her when she crooked her finger at him. He stepped into the elevator with them and the car began to move to the upper floors.

The young man looked at the blonde with disapproval. "You are very frivolous, Olva," he said. "We were told to operate in a state of complete secrecy."

Olva made a face at him and the young man shrugged.

"I like him," she said. "I am sorry that we have to destroy his machines."

Marty tried to speak, to tell her that they did not have to be destructive. He wanted to tell her that the whole world was ready and willing to offer friendship if the chance was available to them, but he found that he could not speak.

The elevator came to a smooth stop at the top floor. It was a vast region filled with computers, analyzers, typing machines. The whole building was filled with various types of machines and as he stood with the invaders, looking around at the conglomerate of sophisticated machines he realized that it was as though information filtered upwards from the basement floors, through endless computers and calculators, to finally erupt, fountain-like, into a welter of dependable logic and filtered facts in this room.

"You come along with us," the blonde girl said. She reached for his hand and took it in her own. He could feel the warmth, the delicate pads of flesh in her palm and when she squeezed his hand he stared at her, amazed.

"You don't have to hold his hand," the young man said. He sounded like a jealous boy friend. The blonde gave him a dazzling smile and then she looked around, walking in the broad corridor, still holding Marty's hand. The young man was looking around too. He strode towards the terminal room and seemed to know exactly what he was seeking.

They stood in the doorway to the huge data terminal room admiring the banks of complicated, humming machines. The young man lifted an unusual tool in his hand, swept it slowly from one side of the room to the other and the machines stopped humming, then they began to smoke, and in moments, they became useless blocks of metal. Martin was shocked, affronted and when he thought of the millions wasted in a moment, he felt a surge of anger almost powerful enough to induce a stroke. The urge to speak, to plead, to berate the handsome young people who were doing such great damage was intense, but he was helpless.

The girl was still holding his hand, drawing him along with them as they went from room to room, waving the fabulous mechanisms into silence.

When they were done, they stepped back into the elevator and the car began to move downwards.

Martin was thinking, realizing that they could fashion a new data-terminal room. It would take time, but they could do it. The young man seemed able to read his mind. He turned to stare at Martin.

"All of the machines feeding those upstairs are now useless, too," he said. "That is why we went there first. I am so sorry."

Martin nodded. "I am, too." The fact that he could speak again startled him. The elevator halted at his office's floor. He stepped out onto the carpeting. The girl in the elevator smiled at him. She tilted her head to one side and he sensed again that she liked him. She said, "Good-bye." She raised her hand, waved it and he suddenly was alone, waiting for the elevator to come to get him.

He was trying to remember what he was going to do and it came to him in a moment. He was on his way to the conference room and he had forgotten about it, practically in mid-stride. That was not like him. He wondered if he needed a rest.

He stepped into the elevator and it carried him up to the conference room. The others were already seated at the long, gleaming table, waiting for him.

Nora stared at him, her eyes worried. "It is very quiet all of a sudden," she said. "Haven't you noticed?"

He yawned and that surprised him.

A moment later, a buzzer rasped and when Marty pressed a button on the console in front of him, the company's chief engineer came onto the closed circuit TV screen. He had a look of astonishment on his face.

"I think you'd better come up to the top floor, Marty," the man said. "We've been put out of business. The machines just stopped running and nothing we do seems to make them work."

"That's not possible," Martin said.

"I know. But, it has happened. You'd better come take a look. Maybe you'd all better come take a look."

They all went up to the top floor in the elevator and stood in the silent rooms, watching the engineers as they examined the complicated mechanisms that were now silent, inoperative. Nora stood beside him and glanced at him from time to time as they awaited the verdict from the engineers.

Granville Weber, the chief, came over to them after a while. He wiped his hands on a piece of waste and tossed it into a receptacle usually reserved for paper.

"Sabotage?" Marty asked.

Granny Weber nodded. He was still surprised, still unbelieving. "I can't imagine how it happened, Yet. But some of the parts are actually fused into solid metal. Just like the machines were struck by lightning. We can get new parts, of course, but it will take weeks to rebuild, or replace the machines."

The vast terminal area was cluttered with men, probing, inspecting, making notes on big clip boards. Nora slipped her hand into his and her smile was a bit rueful, sad.

"I guess we can assume that we were on the right track," she said. "Someone wants the computers out of business. And, us, too, I guess."

He shook himself, realizing that he had been woolgathering. He was wearied and that was very unusual for him.

Lily Trumbull looked at him. She had a fierce, truculent expression on her pretty face. "I'll call Orville Corby," she said, "and see if we can borrow the facilities over there."

He nodded. "We'd better see if the equipment on the plane is in order."

"I'll look into it," Dave Trumbull said. He was silent for a time, looking around him at the bustling activity on the floor. Men were checking machines, trying to make them function and it was not accomplishing anything. Granville Weber came back to them again.

"If a bolt of lightning hit the system," he said, "you might expect something like this. Nothing else could do it."

Martin smiled at him. "Something else did do it."

Granny Weber, a skinny little man in a dark suit, scratched his balding head and nodded, obviously baffled.

They went back to the conference room and sat down again.

Dave Trumbull said, "I'll check on the plane and Lily can talk to Orville and arrange for us to use his equipment, if we have to. Then what do we do?"

Martin said, "Maybe it is time for us to begin using our brains. The machines have done as much for us as they could. We can be pretty certain that we have been invaded by aliens, we can assume that they are responsible for the population explosion. Now let's find them. If they are doing all this, and they want to send the babies they breed on this planet to another, they have to have shuttle ships around somewhere to accomplish the task. We should be able to locate those things."

Nora wanted to argue. "Why should we assume that they want to send the babies somewhere? Why not stay right here?"

Martin sighed. He sat at the head of the beautiful table, his hands folded in front of him.

"I just don't know," he said. "If they were going to be that overt about things, why not come right out into the open and reveal their presence? I have a feeling that they are much more intelligent than we, much further advanced, in many ways. If they do not wish to communicate with us, they won't be easy to find. But, that is what we have been hired to do. I guess we'd better get about it."

They began to plot strategy, to assign tasks. Martin decided that he would seek an appointment with Rupert Hayes, the head of the American Medical Association. He was close at hand, the supervisor of the Florence G. Peary Hospital in New York City. The institution was famous throughout the world as the most up-to-date hospital anywhere. For most of its history, it had been the citadel devoted to ailments of the heart, and curing them.

In the recent past, like all of the other hospitals around the world, it had become a maternity mill. And, like all of the other hospitals, too, it was being added onto, with prefabricated rooms and ells being thrown up every day. Thinking about it, Martin, wondered if Warren P. Bowman, head of the Triple-I, had a piece of the construction deals, too. It would not be too much of a surprise to find that he had a piece. Bowman was like that.

They decided that it might be wiser to use the equipment aboard the giant 747 that the institute kept ever-ready at the New York airport, for their further needs of computers.

"Once they discover that the plane's terminals are merely miniaturized duplicates of what has been destroyed," Nora said, "that equipment may be in danger, too."

"We will have to do that best we can," David said. Lily gave him a fond look and a big smile. It was the kind of look one might give an idiot.

"My David is so resourceful," she said.

Nora decided that she would let Marty drive her home, and she would feed him some dinner. Then he could go to see the head of the medical society in New York, afterwards.

The conference came to an end and Nora went to her office to finish up some work that was on her desk. Martin took the elevator to go up and take another look at the devastation that had been wrought amidst his beloved machines. There were technicians at work but Granny Weber told him, sadly, that it would be a long time before the machines worked again. And their clients were complaining.

Martin was shocked to discover that he was trembling. He was filled with rage because someone could do such things, because it was senseless waste, and because it was a desecration of beauty, of sorts. He did think of the computers and the interlocking equipment as beautiful, functioning, entities, a vast, complex network of brilliantly engineered and programmed brains that could collect and distill and analyze and deliver the product of uncorrupted, unadulterated logic. Now someone had made them junk. Almost like murdering an Einstein.

He stood in the bright lights and resolved that someone would pay for the destruction. He didn't know how it would be accomplished, but he was sure that he would get even, somehow.

In the meanwhile, they would use the equipment aboard the big jet. He realized that Nora was suddenly beside him. She was watching him, a look of great empathy on her pretty face. She put her hand into his and then he turned to look at her and he could see the warmth, the deep affection for him in her big blue-green eyes. The urge to reach for her, to embrace her, to kiss her, was almost overpowering. He noticed the men hustling and bustling around in front of them and gave up his notion.

They got into the elevator and the door closed behind them. Nora turned to face him and he could resist no longer. He pulled her into his arms and he shivered when he felt the silken warmth of her lips beneath his own. She was shivering, too. There was fire and longing and great affection in their kiss and he knew that she would push him away from her too soon. She did it. She stepped back and turned away from him. He could see the brightness in her eyes, the whiteness in her face.

The elevator halted at the ground floor and they stepped out onto the shiny marble lobby, then walked out onto the coarser concrete of the parking area. Nora led the way to her car and he held the door for her as she got in. He walked around the car

38

and got in. He noticed an exceptionally pretty blonde girl in pink shorts and a matching halter. Her eyes were remarkably beautiful, filled with a rather soft luminescence. The girl looked at him and smiled. He smiled, too. The handsome young man with her seemed to be a bit annoyed.

Martin got into the car beside Nora. He closed the door and looked toward the spot where he had seen the girl. He had the odd, ridiculous feeling that he had seen her before. It didn't matter, though.

When he looked for them again, they were gone.

CHAPTER TWO

They were still in the underground of the parking area when they heard the explosion, muffled only slightly by distance. He slowed the car and turned to look at Nora. She looked startled, a bit worried.

He turned the car around and headed back. On their way back to the area that they had just left they could hear the screams of sirens in the distance. He tried to hurry, worried about being overrun by the approaching siren-blasting vehicles. They rounded a turn and came upon total devastation and a crowd of curious people.

"It was your car," Nora said. Her face was very white and she was trembling as she stood with him at the edge of the crowd, looking at the ruins of several other cars that had been parked close to his. He had his arms around her and he held her tightly to him, hoping to stop her shivering.

She twisted to look up at him. "Someone tried to kill you, Marty," she said. "They actually want you dead."

"We must be a threat to them," he said.

Someone said, "Thenna hates you. He thinks I like you. He will do his best to destroy you."

He looked around and saw no one who could have spoken to him so clearly. The words were in his mind but no one had said them. He shook his head, trying to clear it.

The service vehicles arrived; police cars, fire trucks, ambulances, all with sirens blaring, magnified to deafening sound in the subterranean garage. When they came to a halt and the sirens died, the silence was astounding.

He and Nora stood at the outer edge of the crowd and watched as the firemen and the police began their work. He had his right arm around Nora's waist and suddenly there was a warm, soft hand in his dangling left hand. He turned to look, to see who it was. There was no one near him, he saw nothing, but he was holding a human hand. It had to be illusion. He shrugged and gave Nora a quick squeeze.

"Let's go," he said. Nora nodded.

They got back into her car and he drove them out of the bowels of the garage. A traffic cop was at the entrance to the parking ramp, keeping new people from getting in. He blinked at Marty, and, recognizing him, waved him into the stream of outside traffic.

"Kaspin wants you dead, too," a voice said. He heard the words clearly and he glanced at Nora, wondering if she had spoken. She was silent, staring out into the gathering twilight.

"Did you ever hear of anyone named Kaspin?" he said.

Nora turned to look at him. She shook her head, slowly.

"No. Why? Should I have heard of someone with that name?"

"I don't know. Someone just told me that Kaspin wants me dead. I heard the words clearly in my mind, but who could have spoken them?"

Nora lit a cigarette. She handed it to him and lit another for herself. She put the car's lighter back into its niche and settled back against the seat.

"Perhaps the aliens are contacting you telepathically."

"Why me?"

Nora reached out to press a button and a newscaster broke the silence, ". . . the drought continues in Western Europe and as crops wither and die, there are food riots in India and China. Stores and markets are the victims of the looters as all edible foods are rapidly disappearing from the public stalls. . . ." She punched another button and found a local newscast.

" . . . . has been released by Senator Randy Mapes' office. Speaking to a press conference held this morning after his interview with the legendary Martin James, the senator revealed that the United States Government has engaged Martin James and the entire resources of his institute to deal with the baby boom. According to the senator, it is the feeling in government that Martin James and his machines can be helpful in locating and identifying the elements or the people responsible for the strange events that have become a new and frightening part of out future and our present existence. Speaking rather forthrightly, Senator Mapes stated that the constant increase in human births must be halted as quickly as possible.

"Shortly after the senator's conference, Warren P. Bowman, head of the Triple-I, held one of his own."

A cartridge was inserted then and the voice of Warren P. Bowman thundered at them from the loud speaker . . .

"Any attempt to alter the flow of human life and its inception as we know it today must be stopped," Bowman said. "The heavy traffic in abortions, the constant attempts to find and eradicate the source of our new supply of infants, must be stopped. The government and its so-called servants are now very close to murder. We here at the Institute of Infantile Interests want to go on record as opposing any attempt to interfere with the birth and natural development of children, wherever it takes place. We shall resist, constantly, any attempt to interfere with or to control nature's most noble process." Warren P. Bowman took a deep breath and they could hear it whistling in the radio. Then he began one of his long-winded, pontifical diatribes, aimed at a cruel government that wanted to put an end to one of nature's finest activities. Nora turned him off. She sighed.

"So everyone knows what we are doing now," she said.

"It doesn't matter. Maybe it will help."

"How can it help?"

He crushed his cigarette out in the dashboard ash tray. He shrugged. He didn't know, really. It showed, too.

"We will go to your place and have a bite. While you are fixing it, I'll call David and Lily and ask them

43

to air a bulletin asking anyone who sees anything suspicious to call in and notify us immediately. If we have been invaded by aliens, they have to come out into the light of day sometimes, even if only to become acclimatized to our environment. And, if they do intend to send the crop of infants they are responsible for into another world in outer space, they have to have some sort of container to handle them. Sooner or later, evidences of their presence must show up."

"I think we've just seen some evidence of their presence," Nora said. "And while you are talking with David or Lily, you can tell them that I am going to New York with you. I can snoop in the hospital while you are busy with Doctor Rupert Hayes."

He looked at her, sensing the growing fear in her. Fear was beginning to develop in him, too. He was trying to deal with unknowns and dangers that were incomprehensible and that could unnerve anybody. He knew that he would have to hold onto his courage and show a brave face for everyone to see. Especially Nora.

There was room to park in front of Nora's apartment house. They went inside and she began fixing steaks for them while he used the phone to call David. He was still at the office, somewhat disturbed by the destruction of Marty's car.

"Why would they want to kill?" he asked.

"They must be vulnerable, somehow. They must be afraid that we will find them. I'm sure that they are responsible for the sabotage of the computers and the teletypes. And, you know, of course, that Nora and I might have used my car. Or I could have been in it alone." He paused and a thought occurred to him. "Did you ever hear of anyone named Kaspin or something like that?"

"Never," David promised to talk to the networks and ask their cooperation in airing a number that people could call to report anything that they thought warranted investigation. "In spite of our sophisticated systems and computers all over, I'll bet that the invaders are exposed by some average citizen. If there are invaders."

Martin didn't argue. It was difficult for him to believe that Earth had been invaded, too. David had a long list of things to report. Many of the institute's employees and technicians would be working around the clock now, tracing down leads, collecting and analyzing the findings of agencies everywhere that were attempting to identify or isolate the new enzymes or germs that had changed the gestation period in humans. Or to find the virus or germ that had turned the whole world into a massive breeding farm.

After listening to all of the things that David ane Lily were busy with, Martin became decidely impressed by the efficiency and industry of his associates. He promised that he would keep in touch when he and Nora went to New York and then he put the phone down.

Nora was busy in her kitchen. He went out to stand, leaning against the countertop and watch her. She moved over to the sink and flashed him a quick, harried grin. He reached for her and she was in his arms, her slender form trembling.

He kissed her lips and she was stiff and unyielding, as, usual. He yearned to feel her lips move against his own with the same fervor.

She pushed him away and looked at him. Her eyes were filled with tears and there was a wild, not quite calm look on her face. He had the feeling that she was busy hating him.

"Nora," he said, quietly, "don't look at me like that. I love you. You know that I do. Why can't we behave like other people who are in love."

She shook her head and tears splashed onto him.

"I won't love you," she said. "I won't."

He sighed and tried to embrace her again. She fled, backing up against the other side of the kitchen wall.

"Stop it, Marty," she said. "We won't get anywhere. I am not going to be led into that trap. Love and marriage and kids and that scene. I've told you so often, that is not for me. I like my work, I am good at my work. Now leave me alone and let me do my work. Without all of the biological fireworks and that sort of nonsense."

Gravely, he said. "You think that love and marriage and having children are all nonsense?"

Just as solemnly, she said, "It is if you don't want them."

He refused to give up easily. "I love you. You know it. What do we do about that?"

She shook her head, denying his words. "You think you love me, but you don't. You love all of those fabulous computers and teletypes and all the rest of it. The institute is the only baby you will ever want. Or need.

"We spend so much time together, we work together well and we are good friends. Please don't try to make any more out of it. Please, don't."

He reached for her, drew her into his arms. He held her tightly, then he bent his head, kissed the warmth, the silkiness of her lips. She shivered and he felt the merest quiver in her mouth. He let her go and she stepped back, gazing at him with a wide-eyed stare.

"Whatever you say," he said. "We'll do it your way."

Twin tears squeezed from her eyes and slid down her cheeks.

He wanted to say things to her, things that would make her feel better but he did not know what to say. He did not know why she was weeping and he was sure that she did not know either.

"I'll fix our steaks," she said. She turned away from him and began tearing at a head of lettuce, fixing salads for them. He did think she was being unnecessarily vicious with the lettuce.

"You go and see what's on the news," she said. "By now I guess it is well known that you and your machines are after the people responsible for the babies."

They ate their dinner in the living room in front of the TV set and an awkward silence developed. The news was pretty much up to date. There were pictures of the wreckage of his car and there were pictures of the engineers at work trying to repair the damage that had been done to the terminal computer banks.

He wondered why Dave had permitted the newspeople in the sacrosanct computer room. Ordinarily, the institute and its people tried to avoid publicity. Dave had to have good reason to let the news people see the damaged machines.

Nora suggested a possible explanation. "Dave probably wants the vandals to know that they succeeded and that we are not able to use the mechanical brains any more. Maybe now they will stop."

"Maybe," he said. He looked at her and she met his gaze. She shrugged, slightly, tilting her head.

"Sorry about that," she said, "but that's the way I am."

He said, "Guess so. But, I'll keep trying."

Her smile widened and became a dazzling thing. "Isn't that nice?" After that, the awkwardness was behind them.

He wondered if he had spoken truth when he told her that he loved her. He was sure that he was in love with her and had been for a long time, but, everyone was experiencing extremely romantic notions these days. It was something in the air, or the water, or the food supply. Everyone knew about it so he should have been prepared for his outburst of passion. Nora seèmed to have been prepared to cope with it. He sat a few feet from her and watched her and when he felt the rising tide of a brand-new passion rising within him, he turned away from her and watched the TV set instead.

They put the dishes into the dish washer and Nora made a tour of the place, making sure that the apartment was neat and tidy. She knew that they could not know how much time would elapse until they saw her place again.

They went downstairs, deep into the bowels of the building and got onto a shuttle car that would whisk them in seconds to Central Station, a gleaming complex of shops and restaurants and newstands. Marty got tickets for them, an attendant locked them into their seats on the tube train. A few minutes later, they felt the queasy, sliding motion as the tube train eased into its supersonic speed. Marty thought it felt a bit like an elevator on its side. They were getting out in New York City's Mid Town Station a few minutes later. Hundreds of others were getting out too and the bustling anonymity of the tube trains was what he needed at the moment.

After all of the publicity on the TV and the radio, he might have been mobbed by news people and others if he and Nora tried to take a plane. The tubes were about as fast, anyway, and because they were the poor man's way to travel they were always too busy moving people in that mileau to be concerned about anything else. He helped Nora out and they flowed into the crowd that was filling up the elevators.

It was nighttime in New York in April and the

48

softness and warmth of spring was in the air. They walked the few blocks to the huge hospital complex and as they got closer to it, the hustle and bustle of a baby factory was evident. Women with bloated bellies and hurried steps were flowing into the front doors of the hospital, and Martin knew others were being helped inside at the emergency room's admission desks. And, in hidden corridors, the constant flow of females seeking abortions went on, day after day, night after endless night.

Martin and Nora went inside and no one challenged them. The hospital was virtually in a state of siege. There were nurseries everywhere they looked and some women were delivering their infants without help, when it was forced upon them, screaming in sudden pain as the actual birth progressed.

They went to one of the portable admissions desks and the women behind the counter were busy with phones and speaker systems, paging doctors, trying to deal with the hordes of pregnant women who were begging for a bed, help in delivering their child.

Martin reached out and touched the arm of a tall, skinny nurse. She flashed him a harried glance and shook her head.

"You'll just have to wait your turn," she said. "I'm sorry."

"I'd like to see Doctor Rupert Hayes," Martin said.

The girl looked at him, actually saw him. Her eyes widened and her mouth dropped open. "You're him," she said. "On the TV."

Martin nodded. The girl waved toward the distant recesses of the corridor.

"His office is down the hall," she said. "You'll see. Just go in and wait. I'll tell him you are here."

Martin said thank you. He reached for Nora's

hand and they began threading their way through the clutter of women in the foyer waiting to be admitted or delivered.

"This is bedlam," Nora said. "I've never seen anything like this."

They walked along the wide corridor and found Doctor Hayes' office at the far end. They went in and the front office was occupied by a bright-eyed girl in big glasses and a stark white uniform. She had long dark hair and a quick, attractive smile.

"I've already put out a page for Doctor," she said. "He should be along momentarily."

Nora sank down on a long couch and he settled in one of the big leather chairs.

"Doesn't he ever rest?" Martin said.

The girl gave him a probing look. He realized that he had probably asked a stupid question.

"No one rests," she said. "Not these days."

She was working at a teletype machine and she went back to what she had been doing. She touched a button and a TV screen in front of her began working again. The screen was filled with names and pertinent information about recent births. She was monitoring the teletype as it recorded the names and other information and filed it all somewhere on tapes in the hospital's system of computerized records. They were watching the process when Rupert Hayes, head of the American Medical Association, superintendent of the famous Florence G. Peary Hospital, walked in and smiled at them. He was in his green uniform and he had obviously been working. He took his mask off as he walked toward them and reached for a cigarette from the box on the girl's desk. He lit one with the lighter, put the thing down again and crooked his finger at them. They followed him into the private sanctum beyond.

They shook hands and the doctor smiled at Nora.

50

He sat down and waved them into chairs, too.

"It is good to see you, Martin," the doctor said. "I've been hearing great things about you. I hear, for instance, that you are going to put a stop to this crazy glut of babies we are having at the moment. I'm glad. I'm getting just a bit fed up with babies. By the way, I heard, too, about the trouble at your place. We knew that something was wrong, of course, as soon as we lost our umbilical to your center. How bad is it?"

Martin sighed. "Total, I think. The engineers are working on it now. But Nora and I thought we might start our investigation with you. All of the medical information available so far should have become centered here."

Rupert Hayes smiled and it was a rueful, twisted thing.

"I'm afraid we are too busy bringing babies into the world right now. I've heard from hospitals everywhere and they are all experiencing the same land-office business in babies. Why it is like this now, no one knows. We in the medical profession seem to have lost control of the situation."

Nora sat up straight. She reached into her purse and got out cigarettes. She raised her brows questioningly, seeking permission and the doctor smiled at her. "Go ahead," he said.

He was a tall, slender man, nearing sixty now, Martin knew, and aside from his indisputable skill as a surgeon, he was a very bright mind. Probably, Martin supposed, in the not too distant past, Doctor Hayes would have had a Phi Beta Kappa key. In these times he simply had lots of work.

"What can you tell us about your end of the problem?" Martin asked. "We are hoping that we can talk with you and get some idea of where we start our investigation."

Doctor Hayes shook his head. "I'm sure you've

gotten everything that we have learned from the teletypes before they went out." He folded his hands on the desk in front of him and a thoughtful expression was on his face.

"These are entirely new biological procedures we are dealing with now. A three-month period of gestation seems remarkable, unbelievable, but that is the way it is. And, these infants are not really infants in the true sense of the word.

"A day or two after birth, these babies are sitting up, they walk within a week. They are strong, healthy children and they grow and develop very quickly. So far as I know, not one of them has talked yet. But I suppose that we can expect that any day now. The firstborn child is being carefully monitored. He is not quite four months old. But you know all of this.

"We seem to have established that the births are very easy for the mothers, very little pain, and recovery is astonishingly quick. The womb and the birth canal are restored to their original condition with unbelievable speed. And, the women regain their figures rapidly, too. These are factors we would like to keep in the future."

Martin sat back in his chair. He gazed at the doctor, in silence for a moment.

"Can you accept the notion that all of this is being done by some alien force? Or people?"

Doctor Hayes spread his hands. "At this moment, I'm willing to believe anything."

Martin's beeper sounded and the rasping sound startled them. Martin smiled apologetically at the doctor. He pulled his beeper out, which was really a two-way radio. A tiny red light, hardly larger than the head of a pin, was glowing in one segment of the tiny dial. He switched over to line up the channel and spoke.

"Martin here." It was the jet calling. One of the

engineers was monitoring the equipment and he was excited.

"We have reports of an earthquake in a small town in California. We answered a request to monitor from one of our local offices on the coast. Several buildings have been leveled and when the earth shifted, a crevasse opened up and they have found a long metal cylinder buried outside of the town.

"This thing is about a block long and when they got inside, they found that it is lined with tiny incubaters like they have in the hospitals. Thousands of them."

"Thousands of them?" Martin said. The others were listening, doubting, too.

"This thing is really big," the man on the beeper said. "We figured we'd better find you and tell you."

"Thank you," Martin said. "You tell the crew to get ready to take off. We are going to take a look at this new development."

"Yes, sir," the voice on the beeper said. There was a moment of silence, then the man said, "I'll need the password, sir."

"Bingo," Martin said. He shut the beeper off and put it into his pocket. Doctor Rupert Hayes stood and walked out with them.

"Good luck," he said. "Keep in touch." He went through the door with them and walked with them in the wide corridor. "I'm sorry I could not be more helpful," he said, "but I am beginning to hope that we are going to find out what we are up against. I have a great deal of faith in you and your machines."

Martin grinned at him. "They ruined our machines," he said.

Doctor Hayes shrugged. "I have faith in you," he said.

They shook hands with him in the hospital's lobby

and the hectic, frantic parade of swollen women was still going on. The noisy, shuffling crowd was a stark fulminating morass of women, in shoddy clothing, looking unkempt, desperate under the glare of the hospital's white lights and equally white walls.

The admission nurses were busy, pressing patients' palms to admission blanks, while orderlies hovered to wheel the too-ready women off to the waiting delivery tables. Martin watched for a moment, then he and Nora went out into the night and headed for the cab stand.

The sidewalks were crowded and cabs were pulling up into the unloading zones and pregnant women were getting out.

A very pretty blonde girl with exceptionally lovely eyes was waiting for a cab, too. She turned to smile at him and he smiled back. A cab drew up and he expected her to get into it.

The blonde shook her head, slowly and stepped back. He and Nora got into the cab. He turned to call out his thanks to the golden girl but he could not find her.

She had disappeared.

CHAPTER THREE

The taxi took them to the midtown airport shuttle complex and they got into another tube train, strapped themselves in and got comfortable just before the warning buzzer sounded. The buzzer would not work until everyone's seat belt was fastened, and in a few seconds, usually less than sixty, the shuttle began to slide off into the subterranean tubes that crisscrossed beneath the busy city. In moments they were in the airport's tunnels, opting for the V.I.P. area and their own private car that would be waiting to drive them out to the huge jumbo jet, a recently modified version of the huge passenger carrying jet that had first gone into service many years earlier. It had proved to be an efficient people mover and the newer versions were three times as large as the first prototypes. Powered by the intense heat generated in a radium cell, the modern ships were the fastest and safest aircraft at the moment. The institute had three of them in the fleet, the one they were preparing to board now in New York's Metropolitan Airport, one in Paris, and another one that plied between Russia and China and India. All of the big airships operated with the cooperation of the nations whose airspace they traveled in, but the planes were used for peaceful purposes only and this had become well known.

Each of the giant ships was a complete, sophisticated data processing center, usually tied in with the main computer banks in Washington, but those were out of commission now. Martin was worried about the other centers now, the ones that were in the planes and the centers that they bled for information. He suspected that the forces that had destroyed the nerve center of his organization could easily ruin the equipment that was aboard the jumbo jets.

He squeezed Nora's hand as they hurried to board the big plane that was waiting for them. She turned to stare at him.

"We'd better hurry," he said. "If they know that the planes are data-processing centers, too, they may destroy them. Let's get out of here."

They stepped into the portable elevator and it lifted them up into the big jet's reception area. The giant plane, almost as large as a skyscraper, was humming with an eagerness to be airborne and with personnel busy at their tasks.

56

Nora moved over to the receptionist's desk. She smiled at the girl and pressed the palm of her right hand on the identification plate. A light on a panel behind the desk glowed and Nora moved over into the area where the cleared personnel waited to be admitted to the inner regions of the plane.

Martin went through the identification procedure, too, and as soon as the clerk on the desk energized a locking system, he and Nora went through a doorway and moved onward toward the forward compartments and his private quarters.

They settled down in a large living room and Martin used a switch to open a line to the cockpit.

"Let's get out of here as soon as we can," he said.

The ship's captain answered him. "We've got a priority clearance. Sit down, buckle up and we'll go."

He grinned at Nora. She was already sitting in one of the movable chairs. He sat down in one close to her. He got his belt fastened, then he pushed the switch that locked the chairs where they were. It was a powerful magnetic system that allowed the living room furniture to be moved around when desired, but when the plane was landing or taking off, the magnets locked the furniture securely to the metal, carpeted flooring.

They felt the jet moving and Nora turned slightly to look at him. The plane was bouncing around a bit as it trundled its way out to the runway and takeoff.

"We'd better check the terminals here as soon as we are in the air. These banks have been getting the same feed in that the other machines were getting. We can become updated very easily. If these machines have not been damaged, too."

"We would have heard about it by now."

A moment later they were in the air and the ship's captain announced it. They released their seat belts and walked toward the forward compartments.

These were enormous rooms, many of them filled with computer banks and teletype machines and tape-recording machines. Typewriters were clattering and the machines were all working smoothly, efficiently. There were at least a dozen people working in the big room, monitoring the machines, heeding the bells that would ring on one machine or another as certain items of information were fed through and required special attention because the machines had been asked to provide the information, either from memory banks or the flow of input that was constant and up to the second.

Suddenly, bells and sirens began a noisy din all over the plane. Nora hurried over to scan the print-out that was showing on one machine.

The flight commander came on the intercom. "We've got a bomb aboard," he said. "The alarm system became alerted when the bomb became active."

Martin sighed. He was looking at the flashing wall lights and he was able to think a bit more clearly when the technicians silenced the alarms. The sudden relative stillness was almost deafening. Nora was frightened and it showed.

"Now we know," she said. "They know about the planes."

"We'd better warn the others." He touched a button on a wall panel and spoke to the commander. "What can we do?"

The chief pilot answered promptly. "Our bomb technicians heve checked the device. They report that it seems to be a nuclear bomb with a timing device. I have requested permission from the aviation flight control regional command authorities to change course. We will head out over the sea and jettison the bomb. If we are lucky, we have that much time. Everyone sit down and buckle up. We will head for the open sea in a hurry."

58

Martin sat down and Nora and the others did, too. There were special chairs for the purpose in front of the machines. "What do our experts say? Do they give us a fair chance?"

The commander sighed. They could hear it on the speakers.

"We just don't know. Our guys have never seen a bomb like this. And, we go along with the idea that we have been invaded by aliens from space and they have their own plans. We may live through this, maybe not. I've got the throttles wide open. Sit tight and pray."

The speakers shut off and Martin sat worried, wondering if the giant ship would disintegrate at any moment. He was especially concerned about the people aboard. He did not know the exact number of people on duty at the moment but it was always a great number and he worried that they could die because of him and his computers. It was not something palatable to contemplate. He wished that there was something that he could do, but he knew that the technicians that were on board would do the best they could.

A bomb aboard the plane was not an unusual occurrence. When his institute had gained prominence and the news media gave them great fame and too much coverage, probably, the planted bomb became an occasional threat to the continued existence of the institute and its possessions. There had never been an actual explosion because the danger was predictable and the aircraft personnel rounded up bomb squad technicians. Many of them were moonlighting from jobs in police departments.

In this instance, no one seemed to know anything about the bomb that was on board. Only that it had to be got rid of quickly. He opened the curtains at the nearest porthole and looked out into the darkness of great height. It was a pointless thing, really, because he could see nothing. The sensation of great speed was alive and thrumming in the huge aircraft. He glanced at some of the wall instruments and saw the thin red line flowing smoothly across a tiny screen. That meant that they were already in supersonic flight and he could establish their exact speed by touching a button beside the screen and asking for a readout. He didn't bother doing it. It amazed him when he discovered that he was sitting beside Nora, holding her hand, distressed by the look of terror that was in her face. The others in the room were in their seats, silently waiting, wondering, hoping. Some of them were praying aloud.

The plane leveled out and then was steady in flight. Marty got out of his seat. He helped Nora out of the straps that restrained her.

"Let's go up front," he said. "If we don't make it, it won't really matter much where we are when it goes."

She nodded. He glanced around him and saw that the panels were all in working order and the speed indicator showed a flat thin line which meant that they were still streaking through the sky in a hurry. The people who worked in the compartment were all strapped in, all praying, preparing to meet their god in their own way.

He began walking forward, toward the main flight office. The doorways that they went through were sliding panels and they found people seated, strapped into chairs, a look of dread on all faces. Martin picked up the handiest microphone and spoke into it.

"Ladies and gentlemen, this is Martin James. I know that you are all very worried, frightened. Don't be, until we have to really worry. We know we have a bomb aboard but we are heading out over the sea and every second puts us closer to the time when we can jettison the bomb and let it explode harmlessly in the sea. Please, do not despair. We are in good hands. Just sit tight and hope. We'll be all right. I am sure of it."

He put the microphone back into its receptacle. Nora was looking at him with a sort of utter dread on her face.

"We still have a chance," he said. "I thought they should know."

They continued walking forward until they arrived at the flight command office. He rapped on the door and a pretty girl in a bright red uniform let them in. The three pilots were in their seats, one handling the throttles for the engines, the flight captain monitoring the computerized controls that actually flew the plane. The other pilot was off duty, checking their course with one of the navigators. There were at least ten crew in the front office but there was a large opening in the plane's floor and a stairway leading to the deck below. The action was down there, Martin knew. Nora took a cigarette from one of the stews and sat down. Everyone in the front cockpit had a drawn, sweaty look and when Martin glanced at the captain, the man, a nice-looking young fellow with rimless glasses and a nervous grin, shrugged, eloquently.

"We've got a chance," he said. "We need three more minutes on this course, at this speed and we can jettison the package. We don't know what kind of a bomb it is, our guys have never seen anything like it. They are down there, getting it into position to be dropped. In three minutes we will be so far at sea that the bomb burst won't do any damage ashore, presumably. Our problem is staying alive for the few minutes we need."

Nora dropped into one of the chairs in the wide, living-room-sized-cockpit. Martin fastened her seat belt for her. She was shaking too much to be effective with her fingers. She was white faced as she looked up at him and her smile was ghastly.

"They really want us dead," she said.

He didn't answer her. There was really nothing he could say that would assure her comfort. Like everyone else in the plane, probably, he was counting the seconds until the required time had passed. The communications officer was busy with his equipment, talking with the Coast Guard people, explaining the situation aboard the plane, explaining, too, that the bomb would be jettisoned in a certain longitude and latitude and all ships in that area should prepare for stormy weather.

Noticing that Marty was watching and listening, the communications man turned away from his microphone long enough to say, "We will be high enough to minimize concussions that might occur on earth, but we have to warn any aircraft that might be around, too."

They got responses in seconds. The sky was clear and there were no ships in the area. They were heading away from the usual sea lanes. The chief pilot, glanced at his watch and then held up his hands. He had his fingers crossed. He spoke to the men in the compartment below.

"We can let it go now," he said. "Get up here."

Three young men came running up the stairway, coming up out of the ship's belly. They were white, frankly scared.

"Everybody sit," the flight commander said. He began working with controls on the panel in front of him. Marty sat down in a chair that was close to Nora's. He fastened the seat belt and then reached out to take her hand and hold it. She flashed him a look of gratitude.

"We will come out of this all right," he said. "I'm sure of it."

She didn't answer him. The flight commander touched a button and then sat back to watch the TV screen. The closed-circuit system showed the bomb, a round ball the size of a basketball, sliding out of the plane's gaping belly. The bomb bay doors began to close.

"Bombs away," the pilot yelled. "Now let's get the hell away from here."

They felt the huge plane lurch as the controls changed its course abruptly. They settled into a new pathway and the people aboard began to relax.

One of the young men who had been working on the bomb was looking at his wrist watch. He began to count.

"Ten, nine, eight, seven, six, five, four, three, two, one."

A moment later the huge plane was flung high into the sky and it was bouncing and twisting and flopping, helpless in the throes of explosion. After the initial frenzy, the plane settled down but it felt like it was rolling over boulders and the ship shuddered and shook with a violence that threatened to tear it apart. And then it was calm, and smooth and the plane was again on level flight. The pilot was watching his controls and he reached forward to flick on the cabin microphone.

"We're all right now. We can all relax. We are now on our way to the West Coast. In safety, we hope."

Marty spoke to the chief bomb expert. "How could you know when it would detonate?"

The man, still a bit shaken, lit a cigarette. He sat down and sucked smoke deep into his lungs. His hands were trembling and he was not at all ashamed of his state.

"An educated guess," he said. "While we were getting it into position to be dropped, it began making a different sort of noise. We assumed that the change might mean that it would explode in one minute. We guessed exactly right."

Bleakly, Martin said, "I guess we have to realize that these aliens are hostile and quite willing to kill. I'm sorry about that. I guess that we all are. I know I've always hoped that aliens would be friendly. It would seem that such a hope was not realistic."

The chief pilot was making some calculations on a small computer. He twisted in his swivel chair to smile at Martin.

"Touchdown in San Francisco in forty-seven minutes," he said. "That is, if nothing else happens."

Marty nodded. "I'll be in the terminal room if you want me. Come along, Nora. Let's find out what the machines are saying now." He held his hand out and Nora took it. He helped her to her feet and they went out of the flight-control office.

The machines were busy in the main terminal room. He stood beside Nora and began reading some of the floating printouts. Word of their escape from destruction had been flashed around the world and congratulatory messages were clogging some of the machines. One message in particular made him smile.

"During your time of travail," it read, "we here at the Association of Laboratory Logic are glad to offer you our facilities, and, of course, our help in any way such help can be useful." The message was signed, "Orville Corby and Associates."

"Dear Orville," Nora said. "He is always alert to opportunity. We should feed all of our data through his machines and he will be ahead of us very quickly. He knows it, too."

"He doesn't really want to help us. This is just his way of gloating and letting the world know that the aliens have not done anything to put him out of business."

"If they regard him and his institute as a threat to

their safety they will put him out of business, too."

Others came into the room to deal with the information that was being accumulated and digested in the computers. One machine was tabulating the births that were occurring around the world. Millions of infants were being born every twenty-four hours and the computers were struggling constantly to tabulate the births by minutes, by hours.

Martin and Nora were still busy with the computers, still looking for some new or helpful items of information but there were none. They were still watching the readouts when the pilot announced that they were ready to touch down. They sat down in nearby chairs and strapped themselves in. Moments later, they were in one of the portable elevators, leaving the giant airship.

There were people waiting for them. Technicians from the West Coast offices were on hand and there were some government scientists, too. They had gathered from many different directions to join Martin and his technicians in their inspection of the gigantic cylinder that had been exposed by the recent earthquake.

They all piled into a smaller plane and the jumbo jet was hauled off to a far corner of the landing field. While it did seem to be rather exposed, it had to be if it was to continue to function with great efficiency. If it was parked close to a hangar, in one, or close to other structures, the signals that were being absorbed and tabulated by the sophisticated machines within the plane would have been affected.

So the big plane sat out by itself and the people within it continued with their work. As they were circling the airport, while the pilot plotted his course, Martin looked out of his window and felt relieved when he saw the cordon of army men and machines ringing the huge plane. He had asked for armed protection, he was glad that he was getting it.

Nora sat beside him, silent, looking down at the countryside. It was green and pastoral and they were soon looking at cattle grazing in the lush range below them. It was not easy to relate murder and bombs and mayhem to the countryside below. In a few moments, the scene began to change. They were able to see the deep fissure in the earth. Then they were over the shambles of what had been a small village. Shattered buildings were on the ground, nearly everything in sight had collapsed. A long fissure that seemed to extend as long as two or three blocks showed the gleaming surface of a long, bulletlike cylinder buried in the depths of the chasm.

Martin and the others peered at it from the air, then the pilot told them that he was going to try for a landing. Tighten up the seat belts and hold on, it might be a bit ragged getting in. A moment later the plane began its glide, fish tailing with a sickening motion, as it side-slipped towards a clearing.

The landing was surprisingly smooth and when the light plane finally trundled to a stop, a horde of people advanced upon it. A deputy sheriff, resplendent in his uniform, opened the door for them. He helped Nora out and the others in the plane followed in single file.

A heavyset man with a handlebar mustache and fat cheeks stepped forward to grasp Martin's hand and shake it.

"It is a real pleasure to meet you, sir," he said. "I am the mayor here. Rudolph Ormsby, Mayor of Mount Morton. We are an agricultural community here. Or we were. The earthquake sort of put a lot of us out of business. Seems like, anyway.

Martin shook hands and he watched as the others

who had come with him began walking toward the shining thing in the ground. A captain of the local National Guard unit emerged from the crowd.

"I am Major Alan Greir," he said. "I have been ordered to help you in any way. I have my men guarding the cylinder. We were told to wait until you arrived before we try to make an on-the-spot inspection."

Martin nodded. He glanced at Nora. "You want to stay here?"

She shook her head. "I'd like to come along, if I may."

"Let's go."

There were several army vehicles carrying the new arrivals to the site of the cylinder. Midway along its length a trench had been dug, leading down to what appeared to be a doorway in the side of the cylinder. It looked like an aluminum fuselage, gleaming brightly, sitting in utter stillness in the pastoral surroundings. When they reached the entrance to the roadway that had been sliced out of the earth, they found that several armed guards were waiting to discourage the curious.

Martin stood with the military men while they tried to brief him. But they knew very little, only that the earthquake had exposed the long cylinder and subsequent investigation seemed to have established that it was an empty, silent monster, without engines, without any way of getting out of its present resting place. The major felt that Martin should have all available information before he went close to the metal ship. If it was a ship.

"Some of us think it may be a hoax of some kind," the major said. "You know, maybe it was put together for the space shuttles and somebody decided that it was not going to work. So, they dragged it out here and buried it. It could be anything."

Martin and Nora stood and watched as bulldozers began digging the earth away from the long shell, one on either side. It was possible to calculate the dimensions of the long, shiny sleeve and Martin began calculating, working out the figures in his head. Nora was busy, too, but she was keeping the major occupied while Marty made his first inspection of the huge cocoon.

It was about eighteen feet in diameter and a thousand feet in length. It looked like a large portion of an abandoned sewer line. But, Marty knew, it was not a sewer line.

The major suggested that they wait for a bit, until the bulldozers had gotten the earth away from the sides of the thing. Martin and Nora went over to sit beneath a tall shade tree and wait. They lit cigarettes and stared at the cigar-shaped hunk of bright aluminum. Nora gazed around her and then gave him a rueful smile.

"This place is getting crowded," she said. "And new people are showing up all the time."

Cars and people were flooding onto the field and the dirt roadway that was in the distance was clogged with new arrivals.

Several huge trucks loaded with television and motion-picture equipment trundled onto the field, trying to set up as close to the site as possible. The military people chased them to a rather remote distance. They began setting up and young men in sports jackets, holding onto microphones, began talking, taping the commentaries that would accompany their pictures on the late news shows.

After a while, a young lieutenant came to tell them that they could inspect the thing whenever they were ready. He helped Nora up and they walked over to join the major who was waiting for them. They walked down the recently made roadway and waited alongside the shining behemoth. Men that were under the major's command brought electronic listening equipment. They began testing for inner sounds by placing instruments that looked very much like the old-fashioned stethoscope against the metal. They moved from one end of the site to the other and finally announced that there was no sign of life within, no moving parts, either.

There were several projections, buttons, actually, that protruded from the sleek hull. Nora pressed one of them and a doorway opened up in front of her. A panel about six by four feet tilted slightly outward and then slid inside the hull. It moved to one side, out of the way.

There was an opalescence inside. Nora reached for Marty's hand. She held on to it.

"I guess we'd better go inside and take a look," she said.

"I'll accompany you, if you don't mind," the major said.

"Come along," Marty said. He looked back and saw that the military people were putting up ropes, keeping the curious far away from the site. Someone was doing some good thinking.

They entered the doorway and then stood in the midst of the inexplicable opalescence that filled the huge hull. They were standing in a pathway that was carpeted and was about two feet wide. At their feet were rows of tiny, glass-covered cubicles. Incubators. They were in clusters ten by ten and they were on the sides, on the ceiling, everywhere. A pathway, identical to the one they occupied, bisected each row of ten incubators.

"I guess we'd better go forward and see what makes this thing go," Marty said.

"It may be in the rear," the major said. "Perhaps I should take a look there."

Martin nodded. He and Nora began making their

69

way towards the nose of the craft. The interior was immaculate, everything was painted white and as they progressed, Marty realized that the luminescence or opalescence was emanating from the paint. Nora was ahead of him and they found that the craft was a vehicle for carrying incubators somewhere.

There were machines in the nose of the craft. One wall was lined with computers or machines that looked very much like computers. There were metal boxes and strange-looking machines lining the walls. Martin began inspecting some of the weird-looking equipment. He was busy poring over a small square box that seemed to be an oblong of metal. But, like everything else it was a glistening white.

The major came up behind him and Marty jumped, startled.

"I closed the door," the major said. "I thought you'd want complete privacy until you are finished with your inspection."

"Anything in the other end?"

The major shook his head. "No," he said. "Just those tiny cubicles. There must be thousands of them."

"Yes," Martin said.

He was studying the panels on the wall when a sudden sharp sound echoed in the huge shell. A humming sound began and then lights were flashing and running on the panels.

"Something's happened," the major said. "The whole ship is alive. Now what?"

Nora was holding her arms folded across her chest. She began to rub her arms and then she shivered.

"It is cold in here," she said. "Awfully cold."

"We'd better get out of here," Martin said, quietly. "This gadget is apparently the controls to regulate the temperature in here. It is set for one hundred and twenty-seven degrees below zero. So now we know. Wherever this ship is going, it is designed to carry a cargo that is frozen."

"Cryonics," Nora said. Martin nodded.

"Just how cold would that be in metrics?" the major said.

Martin shook his head. "I never studied metrics," he said. "I know that they tried to force that system back in the seventies but they had to give up on it when people wouldn't accept it. I think we'd better get back to the doorway and get out of here."

Nora was shivering and her teeth were chattering. She was rubbing her bare arms again. Martin felt the chill, too.

They discovered that there were many doors built into the side of the ship. But they could not get them opened. There was nothing to use as a tool. Martin took off his shoe and began banging on the hull. He could not dent the metal.

The white-painted interior was beginning to show frost and Marty took his coat off so that Nora might try to keep warm with it.

Their breath became wavering white columns in front of them and the opalescence began to fade. Martin tried to say something to Nora, to reassure her, but his mouth was stiffened and his lips would not work right. The major, terrified, looked at him.

A new and louder humming began and the long ship began to shiver and throb. Martin kept on pounding on the frosted walls but it was evidently futile.

"It looks like we're goin' onna trip," he said, stiffly.

The cold was beginning to penetrate his skin, to burrow deep within his body. He knew that it would be a matter of minutes only until he and Nora and the major were frozen solid.

There was nothing he could do about it.

The major, moving slowly, got his cigarette lighter out and a package of cigarettes. He looked like the man who asks for a smoke just before the firing squad destroys him.

"D-d-d-d-d-don't," Marty said. He plucked the lighter from the man's fingers. "You can blow us all to pieces."

"D-d-d-does it m-m-matter?"

Marty handed the lighter back. Shaking, the major put a cigarette into his mouth. He flicked his lighter and nothing happened. He kept trying. Finally, he flung it from him and it clattered as it skidded along the frosted passageway.

A new and louder humming began and the huge hull began to move, slowly, easily.

Martin sat down on the edge of an incubator. Nora sat on the floor beside him. She was still shivering, and Martin suspected that he was very close to death. They all were.

He dozed and then consciousness left him.

He wanted to sleep. He was so tired. So awfully tired.

CHAPTER FOUR

It was shortly before lunchtime when Angie, his secretary, told Warren P. Bowman that Orville Corby was calling him on the videophone. He smiled at the girl and pressed the button on his own machine.

Orville Corby's thin, angular face with its deep-set little eyes stared at him from the screen.

"Hello, Orville," he said.

"Warren," Corby said, "I think we should get together and have some lunch. We have to talk."

"What would we talk about, Orville?"

Orville Corby's face became sad, solemn. "You owe me a lot of money, Warren. You made a deal with me to feed your computers all of the information I could get. I've been doing it, but we are having problems with our own machines now."

"You mean that Martin James' machines went out of commission and you can't get information any other way."

"That isn't fair, Warren," Orville said. "We have our sources of information, too, you know."

Warren sighed. "I suppose so," he said. "I'll meet you in The Persian Room at noon. All right?"

Orville said yes. He disconnected and his gaunt, sad face went off the TV screen.

Warren looked at his wrist watch. The picture of a smiling baby was on the dial and the infant's right leg was at the numeral 4 while the left arm pointed to ten. Ten-twenty. The watch was rimmed with diamonds and the baby's eyes were tiny sapphires, the navel a tiny ruby. It was an imposing watch, an impudent piece, really, he supposed, but it had been a gift from one of the baby food manufacturers and he was grateful for it.

He touched a button on the walnut plaque on the desk and his secretary came in, her notebook clutched in her hands. She was a tall girl, a redhead with a remarkably good figure. Warren loved beautiful things and he enjoyed working with the many women who were always involved with him in his various projects. After all, he supposed, *babies* were decidedly women's business.

"What time do I have to meet with the Committee for the Supervision of Children's Television? That's their name, isn't it?" He sat back and smiled his sad smile for the girl. "There are so many. Always so many people."

Angie was properly sympathetic, properly respectful.

"I don't know how you manage to do it all," she said.

"Well, we must do the best we can. These are stirring times. How are your youngsters, my dear?"

Her smile thanked for his interest.

"They are growing like little weeds, of course, and they seem to be happy in the nursery. They are beginning to learn and I am just so proud of them."

"And with good reason, my dear. They are handsome children. Now, what do we have to face today?"

The girl became businesslike again. She consulted her notebook and said, "The committee for supervising children's TV are waiting for you now. I've put them in the conference room and they are busy looking at some of the programs our monitor groups have cited for censure. After your session with them you have a meeting with the advertising rep for Baby Carol Foods. You are open for lunch but I have seven lunch invitations for you."

He shook his head. "No. I'm going to have lunch with Orville Corby. He seems to be a bit upset about things."

Angie waited, smiling. He sighed.

"I'll go along and meet with the supervisory people. Then I'll see Elwood Amory. Shortly after eleven. If you'll set it up, I'll be grateful. After that, I'll have lunch with Orville. We'll be at the Persian Room if you have to reach me."

Angie nodded and went back to her desk. He stood up and walked over to the black-tinted window wall and looked out over the bustling city. He loved the capital, the hustle and bustle of important work and great deeds. He knew everyone who was in government. During his days as a lobbyist he had worked very hard to get acquainted with the people in Congress as well as in the various levels of administration.

Lobbying for the baby-food manufacturers had seemed to be a dead end in those days. There was no place to go. And then he became involved with some of the women's groups fighting for one thing or another.

A pretty girl in Idaho suggested, during a meeting, that there should be some sort of institute devoted exclusively to the needs of children. When Bowman mentioned it to the field representative of the largest manufacturer of baby foods, the man thought it an excellent idea. Two weeks later, financing for the institute was available and the project became a reality.

It always amazed him when he realized that the baby food manufacturers, the toy makers, the children's clothing companies, had all chipped in to help him found and operate an institute that forced them to adhere to the rules of goodness that they often bent a bit.

Little by little, the institute became independent, not needing subsidies any longer. Instead there were fees for supervisions, fees for many things, and the institute and its owner were now very rich, very powerful.

And its seal of approval on a product could mean millions to the lucky manufacturer. It was not awarded without a fee.

He possessed enormous power and enjoyed it. Babies and their needs had become a multibillion dollar industry. And he was its boss. Absolute boss.

It was only fitting that the head of an institute such as the Triple-I should live well. He now owned a lavish estate in the fashionable suburbs. When he first acquired it, he worried that he would be criticized for living off children and their needs.

Instead, he was hailed as the champion of the very young, the dedicated servant, the constantly vigilant sentinel, fiercely protective of the rights of those who needed protection.

He did work hard. He was often in his office late at night, long after the others had gone home, scanning reports, printouts that Angie thought he should look at. He liked to open the drapes at the window wall and gaze out at the brightly lit dome of the Capitol. Somehow, the sight of the government buildings, glowing in the incandescence of the spotlights, gave him a sense of security and well-being that he found enjoyable.

He wished that he could be the one to explain what was happening with motherhood in the world now. He knew that Martin James and his associates had been retained to dig into the matter and he supposed that they would manage to demand a fortune for their efforts.

Martin James was not a friend. He had met the man on many occasions and he did not like him. He was too good-looking, too successful, too secure in his own value to society. And he was not at all involved with babies. Martin James could move about in the world and never wonder what people would think of him. He was top man in the field of computerized research and everyone knew it. Warren hated him, and he wished that he could do something to rid the world of Martin James and his machines.

Angie came into the office to jar him out of his thoughtful contemplation of the world outside.

"The women are waiting for you, sir," she said.

He nodded, and started for the door. Angie waited, making sure that he went on his way. Angie had a mother complex, he supposed.

They were waiting for him in the huge conference room.

The president of the committee was a large blonde girl with big teeth, a wide smile, and an exaggerated sense of her own importance. She came forward, emerging from the cluster of women like a wiggle worm escaping the petals of a rose. She put her hand on his arm and her smile was coy, warm, enticing.

"Doctor Bowman," she said, "it is nice to see you. We have been waiting for you for we have a new list of programs that we want you to eliminate. Immediately. Miss Gorman will give you the list and I will gladly go over it with you."

He sat down at the head of the long conference table and the women nudged and battled each other for seats close to him. He ignored their eagerness to be near him, but he was flattered and they seemed to know it.

"Just Mister Bowman," he said. "I am not yet a doctor."

"I am Mrs. Wilbur Hallman," the boss lady said. "I'm sure you will soon be Doctor Bowman. Perhaps I can arrange a doctorate for you, if you like. The head of a large institute such as yours should be doctor. Don't you agree?"

He showed her his teeth in an insincere grin and she reached out to pat his hand. She caressed the huge diamond on his little finger and stared at it, intently, appraisingly.

He took his hand away from her and put it in his lap.

Miss Gorman, a skinny old maid type, had a long list of TV shows that she thought should be taken off the air. She had a pile of letters and petitions that supported her and her colleagues.

"I will do the best I can, of course," he said, taking the paperwork into his own hands. He pressed a button beneath the table's edge and Angie came into the room. He gave the paperwork to her and she went back to her lair, leaving him alone again with the women.

"How quickly can we expect you to get rid of these programs, Doctor Bowman?" Mrs. Hallman demanded. The others leaned towards him, waiting for his answer.

"It won't be easy," he said. "They fight so hard to keep their little shows. They talk about free speech and things like that. Censorship, you know. It may require an act of Congress to do something positive. But, I try. I want you ladies to know that I do try."

"Of course you do," Miss Gorman simpered. "We are just *so* pleased with you."

They chattered for a time and then he pressed the hidden button twice and Angie came in, properly apologetic because she had to interrupt, to tell him that there was an important long-distance call from the White House. It was a lie, of course.

The women cooed and fluttered like a flock of pigeons when they heard that, but they did leave. He gave them his promise to do what they wanted him to do and then he left the conference room with Angie.

They parted in the hallway and he took the elevator to the thirtieth floor. He emerged in the foyer of Elwood Amory's plush offices. The little blonde girl at the reception desk smiled at him. They were old friends.

"He's waiting for you, Mr. Bowman. You may go right in."

He gave her his magnificent smile, the one reserved for cute and charming underlings. "Thank you, Jenny," he said.

He passed by her desk and pushed a door open and went through it. Two male secretaries were busy at their desks on either side of the wide corridor. They were actually guards, intended to head off and deal with any of the wild, raging mothers who might

79

have gotten that far in their search for the executives of the local office of Baby Carol Baby Foods.

Elwood Amory, a tall slender man with rimless glasses and bright white teeth, was the local representative of the largest manufacturer of baby products. It seemed only fitting that his offices should be in the monolithic citadel of glass and steel devoted to the requirements of children.

Warren liked Elwood. They got along very comfortably and when the institute's testing labs found something not quite right with any of the Baby Carol products, he told Elwood and something was done about the complaint immediately. After the correction was made, the product was awarded the seal of approval from the Triple-I and went on the market to earn millions for its maker.

He nodded at the two young men who might have been football players in another era and went on to Elwood's office. He knew what they would talk about.

The applesauce.

Baby Carol Products had brought out a new applesauce that was partially synthetic. With millions of new babies clamoring for food the demand for baby food products was insatiable. Some of the manufacturers had developed the practice of adding amplifying chemicals to batches of their product. They could take a bushel of apples and turn it into a ton of applesauce, retaining the flavor of the fruit and little else. His lab people had tested the new applesauce put on the market by Baby Carol and found that even the flavor was synthetic. It was mostly soy bean meal and chemical flavoring. His experts raised the possibility of carcinogens being active in the chemical substances.

He had sent a report to Elwood's office and he was

about to issue an order recalling all of the product available. Elwood would try to arrange for postponement. His company could make millions of dollars from the questionable product's sales while the negotiations for its withdrawal were being processed. And millions of infants could be poisoned or made ill.

Elwood was waiting for him, slumped on the base of his spine, his fingers making tents in front of his vest. His eyes, behind the rimless glasses, were alert, watchful. There was a pink check on the desk top. Nothing else.

"Good morning, Warren," Elwood said. He straightened up in his chair and reached for a ciagrette from a package he took from his coat pocket. Warren stood in front of the desk. He read the information on the check. *Pay to the order of Warren P. Bowman, fifty thousand dollars. . . .*

Warren reached for the check. He looked at it while he held it in his fingers. Then he tore it to bits. He placed the pieces in a pile on the desk. Elwood Amory spread his slender manicured hands in surrender.

"I didn't think you'd accept the check," he said.

"I am issuing a recall order for the applesauce this afternoon. I am thinking of assessing a penalty for each can recovered. Your company and the others must realize that the children of the world must be protected. Perhaps a whopping fine would help your executives remember that."

Elwood shook his head slowly. He stood up and walked over to close his office door which Warren had purposely left open. He went back to his desk. He bent down and put a black attache case on the surface of his desk.

"You forgot this the last time you were here," Elwood said. He glanced at the intercom device on his desk. The key was open and he stood for a moment, looking at Warren. "We will recall the applesauce immediately. Will that satisfy you, Warren?"

He nodded. Elwood smiled then. He waved Warren into a chair. The black attache case loomed large, occupying much of the space on top of the desk. Elwood went to the office door, opened it.

"Miss Garrett," he called out, "would you step in here a moment, please?"

The secretary, a chubby girl with bright eyes and a sexy walk, came in and stood waiting for instructions.

"Would you take this out and put it by the door, please? And make sure that Mister Bowman takes it with him when he leaves? He always seems to forget it."

"Yes, sir," the girl said. She picked up the case, held it in her hands. Elwood's fingers scooped up the remnants of the check. He placed them on top of the brief case. "Get rid of that, too, please," he said. The girl smiled, turned and went out of the office. Elwood closed the door behind her. He sat down and closed the key on the intercom with a beautifully manicured fingertip. Then he grinned at Warren.

"You drive a hard bargain," he said.

Warren shrugged. He got out his gold cigarette case and matching lighter. He lit a cigarette and put the case away again.

"If I assessed a per-can fine it would run into millions. Your people are getting away cheaply."

Elwood sighed. He smiled the thin, bleak smile of the harried business man. "We are not complaining. The girl could testify that you destroyed the check we tried to bribe you with. And, you did not leave my office carrying anything. She took it out of here for you." He glared at Warren, not entirely with anger. "Maybe you should give her a piece of it."

Warren laughed at him. "Why don't you have one

of your people return the case to my office? I am on my way to meet our dear friend Orville Corby."

Elwood nodded. He pushed the intercom key again. "Miss Garrett, please have someone deliver that case to Mr. Bowman's office. He is not returning to his office. Not at the moment."

"Yes, sir," the girl said.

Warren gazed at Elwood a bit worriedly. "It's locked?"

"Of course. With fifty thousand dollars in cash in it, you can be sure it is locked. You have your key, don't you?"

Warren nodded. He stood up.

"How quickly will you recall the applesauce?"

Elwood stood, too. He began walking Warren to the door.

"This is Friday," he said. "Suppose we issue the recall order bright and early on Monday morning?"

Warren stared at him. "You will sell millions over the weekend. Millions."

Elwood wore a look of great distress and sadness. "What can one do?" he said, helplessly. "These things happen."

"Sure," Warren said sarcastically, "and you do have to recover the fifty thousand dollars you are contributing."

"There is that," Elwood said, calmly.

They shook hands and Warren stepped into the elevator again. He went to the garage level in the paneled cab and found his chauffeur waiting for him, undoubtedly alerted by Angie. She was such a fine intelligent girl, he thought. Angie had been with him for a long time now and she knew him well. Perhaps he should have married her in the early days before she found the husband she had now. And before he met Amy Driscoll.

He sat in the limousine while the chauffeur guided the car through traffic, heading for the restaurant and he thought about Amy and he knew that he should not think about her.

A beautiful brunette with big, sparkling eyes, Amy was the head of one of the women's militant groups. They were pretty much out of step with the times now because the pendulum had swung far over to the other side and women were in high places everywhere in the world.

In recent years, Amy Driscoll and her organizations had become interested in the rights and privileges of children. At first they had been most concerned with the abused child, then they interested themselves in juvenile delinquents. Amy's group would furnish legal representation for any youngster who was in trouble with the law. And, they had counselors and advisors who were doing good things for the younger generation.

He loved Amy with an unyielding passion and she knew it. Whenever they met she would be kind and considerate and frankly amused by his constant adoration. He suspected that she was much more intelligent than he was. He was honest enough to admit that her beauty always turned his brain to yogurt and he rarely got the chance to explore her mentality.

He wished that he could put her out of his mind forever and the thought of such horror made him shiver. He looked out the car's window at the bustling street and wished he could have Amy Driscoll for his very own forever.

They had dined together often and he had tried to make her realize how very much he loved her, but she did not seem to be impressed. The last time they had talked it had been in one of the very posh restaurants and there was music fed into the private booth. It was very quiet, very intimate and the flickering light of the candles had made her seem impossibly beautiful. Her big brown eyes were twinkling at him and her smile made her lips irresistibly kissable. He stifled the urge to reach for her, to kiss her, to beg her for marriage. He reached out to cover her tiny hand with his own.

"You know I love you, Amy," he said. "I love you so very much. Why can't we be married and have kids of our own like everybody else?"

She shook her head slowly, staring at him with an unusual gravity. Her long brown hair gleamed in the faint light and her cheeks had a touch of translucence that heightened her look of ethereal loveliness. And she was saying no again.

He put his cigarette into the ash tray and noticed that his hands were shaking. She could always do that to him.

"I would worry about the children if I married you, Warren," she said. "You hate children. You really do."

He was astonished. "How can you say that? Children are my life. My whole life."

She shook her head again, slowly. "Perhaps, but you don't know any children that you love or even like. You deal with them collectively. I think if someone brought their kids to the institute and one of them crawled up into your lap you would want to brush him off like lice. No, Warren. You are a big fraud. I like you, of course, and we are friends, but I don't have any illusions about you." She bent and found his ips in the semi-gloom and her kiss was warm and sweet and rather moist. It made him shiver. She sat back again. "Let's talk about the things we must talk about, Warren."

They did talk about the problems she had brought to him and he took her back to her office, finally, and she kissed him lightly, chastely, and went off to her delinquents, probably.

He thought about her comments for days. He didn't think he was a fraud. Not really. A few days later, one of the women's groups sent some representatives to visit with him for interviews and pictures for the media. Some of them brought their infants.

"We wanted our children to meet the one man who spends his whole life thinking of them, helping them," one pretty young mother said. She pushed her baby at him and he took the child into his arms. The baby cried out loudly, protesting, then it began spitting up all over his six-hundred-dollar suit and its diaper leaked all over him, too. He stood, his brave smile frozen on his face. A few days later, Amy brought the picture to him. She had found it in the Sunday paper.

"See how happy you look?" she said, teasing him. "I've seen happier faces on a corpse."

He reached for her and held her and she let him kiss her and he was startled to see that there were tears shimmering in her eyes when he let her go.

"Why do you keep saying no to me, Amy?" he said. "Why?"

She shook her head, her tears bounced onto his cheeks and a strangled sob sounded deep in her throat. She pushed herself away from him. She turned and ran. He sat down at his desk and studied the picture. Amy had left it behind. She had her offices in a building down the street. When he was finished with the paper, he rang for Angie and sent her over to return it.

Lately he had the feeling that Amy was avoiding him.

The chauffeur opened the car door for him and he saw that they were in the parking area beneath the restaurant. He stepped out and walked on the red carpet to the elevator. A moment later he was smiling at the *maitre d'* in the restaurant's foyer.

"Mr. Corby is waiting for you, sir," the man said.

Warren nodded. A pretty blonde in a deep red uniform came to usher him to the table. He found Orville Corby in his own private booth, the one the restaurant usually reserved for him. He smiled at Orville as he slid into his seat. Orville did not return the smile. He looked worried, unhappy.

Warren ordered an aperitif. Orville shook his head when the girl glanced at him for his order. She went away. Warren settled back in the upholstered banquette.

"Orville, how are you?"

"You know how I am. I want my money. You and that institute of yours are very good about collecting your money. You change your attitude when it comes to paying it out."

Warren gave him smile number forty-seven (sad, rueful, but concerned about the rights and privileges of others). Orville had seen it too often to be affected.

"I want money, Warren. I have to pay my people, too, you know. And, you haven't paid us for a long time."

"You haven't done much for us, either, Orville. The data your lines feed us can be found in the newspapers. After Marty James and his people release it."

"We do the best we can, Warren. And, of course, if you like, we can sue."

"Of course you can. Why don't you do that?" Warren Bowman knew that he hated to be threatened, especially by the little excomputer programmer who had become successful mainly because of Warren's patronage.

Orville glared at him with malevolent truculence.

"I will stop in and see Amy Driscoll after lunch and ask her to initiate suit. I know you won't be angry. Business is business and we do what we must do to survive."

Warren said, "Orville, I am teasing you. You

should know that. Your check has been delayed by paperwork and that sort of nonsense. I will ask Angie to find your account and settle it immediately. All right?"

Orville was not too well satisfied. "What does 'immediately' mean?"

Warren spread his hand and smiled up at their waitress as she brought their drinks.

Crisply, he said, "You'll have the check on your desk this afternoon, Orville."

Orville smiled. He spoke to the girl who was still lingering. He ordered a drink, too.

When they were alone, Warren said, "We have to do something about Martin James. I don't care what we do, I just want to make certain that you and your technicians are the ones to find out the answer to the current problem. *I* want to release it."

Orville's thin face brightened and his pop eyes were shiny.

"Marty James's machines are a pile of junk now. They put a bomb aboard that flying data-processing center he owns. The last we heard on the TV, he and his associate, Nora, were on their way to the West Coast to inspect that thing they found out there. What can we do to him that isn't being done?"

"The aliens, if they are here, don't like Marty James. And they are showing their dislike. Maybe we can sort of help them along. Maybe you should get out to the coast and see to it that Marty James doesn't interfere with things. He is trying to stop the birth of infants, Orville. We don't want anyone to interfere with the noble process of birth. And if Martin James tries to interfere, I think he should be stopped."

Orville stared. "Warren," he said, softly, dazedly, "you are talking violence."

Warren smiled his conciliating, affectionate smile.

"That is such an ugly word, Orville, dear friend. I'm sure you can find other words to describe our needs. Martin James is not the indispensable man."

"You are?"

"Yes, Orville. I represent infants, the helpless, the weak ones. Millions and, perhaps, billions of babies have to depend on me to fight for them, to preserve their right to live in safety and comfort. This responsibility I bear gladly and I feel that those who are, in a sense, in my care, must come first. Martin James and his associates have been hired to find the cause of the population explosion and put an end to it. You must not let them do that, Orville."

A pained look flashed across Orville's face. "We have been hired to do the same thing. But by a different agency of the government. The boom in babies must be stopped. No matter what it costs. That's what we were told."

Warren reached out to capture Orville's skinny hand. He squeezed it.

"I am telling you just the opposite, Orville. Take the money and concentrate on Martin James and that pretty girl assistant. Just think what it would mean, incomewise, if your institute was responsible for exposing the whole process of the baby boom, the shortened term of gestation, the new breed of infant that we now have on our hands. Think what it would mean, Orville, if we controlled it all. Millions."

"I'm thinking. But, how can I accomplish that?"

"You discredit Martin James and I'll take care of the rest. Do we have a deal?"

Orville Corby nodded. He held out his hand. Warren took it.

Gravely, with great purpose and intent, they shook hands.

Orville gulped his drink down. He signalled their waitress and ordered another. Warren began studying the menu.

They ordered and the girl went off with the big cards that served as menus. Orville was very white, very nervous.

"Shall I worry about you, Orville? Can you do the things you must do if we are to be rid of Martin James?"

Orville nodded. "I don't have much choice. Do I?"

Slowly, ponderously, Warren shook his head. Really, there was no choice.

CHAPTER FIVE

They left the restaurant together. Orville loved riding in the Rolls and Warren Bowman felt a strong sense of kindness when he invited Orville to ride along. They dropped the skinny little man in front of his office building. He gave the chauffeur Amy's address and settled back in the seat, trying to decide what he would say to Amy. He always had some questions for her to deal with. It was a device, of course, and they both knew it, but Amy never unmasked him.

The chauffeur halted the Rolls in front of the elevator on the parking level of Amy's building. He got out and smiled at the young girl who pressed the button for him. The doors opened and he entered the wood-lined cab. The doors slid closed, he touched the button for the 34th floor and was whisked upwards in seconds. When the doors opened again he stepped out onto the bright orange carpeting that brightened the reception area. A smiling blonde sat behind the big desk.

"Hello, Norma," he said. "You look lovely today. But, I suppose you hear that all the time."

"Never often enough," she said.

"I'd like to see Ms. Driscoll."

"I guessed," Norma said. "You can go right in, if you will."

He found Amy behind her messy desk. She was busy with someone on the telephone and she reached out to switch the desk set off and funnel the conversation into the receiver at her ear. He smiled at her and sat down.

She finished her call and put the phone away.

"Why have you come to see me, Warren?" she asked. She sat up straight and the sight of her beauty very nearly shut off his wind. He dropped his bulk into the visitor's chair and looked at her. She was smiling at him, obviously fond of him, at the moment.

"I enjoy visiting you," he said.

"I am very busy, Warren. You know that. Now what is it?"

He sighed and straightened up in his chair. He was a tall man, a bit too-well fleshed, addicted to black silk suits and start-white linen and diamonds. He loved jewels and he knew that he dressed in a manner some considered flashy. He wore big black spectacles, his bald head shone, but he believed that he presented an appearance of great dignity.

Amy was not a tall girl. She had to sit up straight behind her desk so that she could see over the pile of law books that littered the surface. It annoyed him to suppose that she was probably researching some fine points of law so that she could defend, brilliantly, of course, some unfortunate, penurious miscreant. She would rather work at that than visit with him.

Another thing that bothered him about Amy. She was the great champion of the abortionists. She believed that a woman's body was her own possession to use as she chose and she had been so blatant about it in the courts, everyone knew how she felt about abortion.

She smiled at him and her big brown eyes were twinkling with good humor. "What can I do for you, Warren?"

"If you were to become my wife, you would also become chief counsel for the institute."

She shook her head. "We've been over that before. You know that I think your institute is crooked, you are crooked, too."

He sighed. She watched him intently as he sat down, lit a cigarette. He placed the used match in the ashtray with care.

"Martin James and his people have been hired to find the cause of the new gestation term and the heavy population glut by the government. Orville Corby and his institute have been hired by another branch of the government to do the same thing. I would like you to talk to the president and see if you can arrange for me to be hired directly by the president."

"Why would I want to do that?" Amy asked. "What good would such an appointment do for you?"

He stood up and looked down into her eyes and it was not easy for him to keep his mind on the things he wanted to say to her.

"Orville and Martin James are determined to put an end to the production of babies around the world. I want the president to appoint me and my institute to head off the project. I want to make sure that no one is permitted to interfere with the noble process of birth."

Amy stared at him in perplexity.

"What makes you think I can help you?"

"You can get to the president. After all, you did help her to get elected. And she would listen to you, she would be inclined to heed any recommendation you might make."

Amy shook her head, slowly, positively.

"I would not do that, Warren. And, I don't think you are levelling with me. What are you really after?"

He gave her an unhappy, reproving look. "Our marriage would be a stormy affair. Oh, well . . . The thing is, there is a certain group in Congress that is determined to tax infants, or the people who have them. They think that taxing the parents heavily will discourage the process of having children. And, worse yet, this same group wants to tax everything that a baby needs or uses. For the same reason, of course. That means that the government will send in auditors to go over our books and that means all kinds of problems. I can't have that."

Amy grinned. "They would find out what you've been stealing from the institute. Right?"

"Not necessarily. They might not approve of my bookkeeping, but, there would be other problems. I could not live or work with government supervision and that is what is in store for us if things go on the way they are heading now."

Amy stood up. She faced him with the desk between them. She leaned forward and her lips brushed his in a sweet, amiable kiss. It was totally unexpected and decidedly enjoyable. He tried for more, reaching out to try for an embrace. She backed away from him. Her eyes were wary, concerned.

"I can't help you, Warren. I wouldn't go to the president for something like that. The government wants the quick, multiple births to end, not because there is a sudden hatred for infants, but because the whole world is now flooded with babies and no one can seem to think of anything else. The whole world is preoccupied with babies. But, most people tend to suppose that it is a phase and will end shortly.

"For some reason, not yet explained, the baby boom is upon us but the reasons for it will be discovered and dealt with. Take my word for it."

Almost unhappily he said, "You don't believe that it's aliens?"

"No way. Aliens, indeed." She bent across the desk and kissed him again. "Go back to your work, Warren, and let me do mine."

He didn't see her press a button but her office door opened and her secretary, a tall, dark-haired girl with big glasses, came in and stood, waiting, ready to usher him out. Amy grinned at him impishly, merrily. He said good-bye and left her.

The day was warm and he elected to walk back to his building. The chauffeur drove past him as he sauntered along the busy street. It bothered him to know that Amy was a going concern in her own right, a brilliant attorney who really did great things for her clients. He wondered how he could persuade her to take his frequent proposals seriously.

He had been so sure that talking to her would be productive. She was a good friend to the president. She had worked hard and long to help get Madeline Fremont elected to the country's highest office. Amy could easily have a little talk with her friend and arrange to have Warren P. Bowman and his institute placed in charge of the vast investigative surveys that were now going on.

But Amy wouldn't do it.

It would be so great if he could be put in charge of things. He could be on hand to make sure that the rights and privileges of infants around the world were protected. Too, he could learn the secret behind the new period of gestation and sell pills to accomplish it, if that was the way it was done.

The new mothers snapped back in astonishingly short periods of time. Their bodies regained their normal measurements quickly and women would pay for such knowledge.

He was still thinking about Amy and her perfidy against him when he walked into his own office. Angie was waiting for him, besieged by women who were eager to see him, to talk with him.

He went into his office, settled behind his desk and then told Angie he would see his first appointment. That turned out to be an elderly woman who was determined to put one of the local merchants out of business because he had sold her a crib for a baby she was too old to bear. She had hoped to have a child but the medics had finally told her she was too old. So, she wanted him to get her money back from the merchant.

He told her he would see what he could do. He told Angie to call the merchant, tell him to refund the woman's money or face the anger of the Triple-I. A bit later Angie reported that the merchant would gladly make the refund. Warren smiled and went on seeing people.

Angie brought coffee and Danish into the private office for him and she joined him while they watched the five o'clock news bulletins on the giant, wall-sized screen.

There were others waiting for an audience with

him, she said, but they would wait or come back tomorrow. Since the inception of the new births, the news broadcasts became immensely important and he had begun the practice of taking a half hour for coffee and cakes and the news. Angie was interested, too, so they sat in his private office while the television system brought them up to date.

The dour face of a newscaster stared out at them from the screen. "Food riots are spreading from far-away China to Spain, as troops were called out today to put down the rioters and looters in Madrid. An air lift was inaugurated today to bring water to dry Londoners. The European drought combined with the baby boom has exhausted the public water supply. Planes are being flown from several northern areas of Scotland to bring relief to a dry and parched city. . . ."

"Change the channel," Bowman hissed. "Let's see what's really going on."

Angie punched a button and the newscaster gave way to a picture of a huge plane that had carried a bomb out to sea. There were pictures of the long, gleaming metal cylinder that had been discovered in northern California. The news cameras showed the site and the hordes of people who were flocking to it.

He sat with Angie watching the screen, squirming with a feeling of jealousy or disgust when he had to watch Martin James and his associate, the brilliant Nora Corwin, land at the site. The fawning attention the army people gave Martin James and Nora indicated the esteem with which they were regarded. There was a panoramic sweep of the scene and the ropes that had been strung up around the metal cylinder were shown and the commentator said that people were traveling to the site with the fervor of the devout approaching the scene of a miracle.

"The finding of this strange metallic ship," the commentator said, "seems to represent the first tangible hint that we have had that other beings are now here on earth. When the vehicle was first located, expert metallurgical engineers were called in to test the metal and they report that it appears to be constructed of an alloy that is not like anything known on earth. Our scientists are very much encouraged now that a breakthrough, or at least an explanation of what is taking place here can soon be expected.

"The military people here at the scene are determined to keep the curious away from the new find, until our scientists have had a chance to examine this weird, cigar-shaped cylinder. We will keep you informed as developments take place. Now we return you to the studio news program."

The balance of the news program was dominated by the new events, the cluttered hospitals that were being turned into maternity mills now, many of them previously unavailable for maternity cases, the long lines in the welfare agencies as the government tried to keep abreast of the growing need for food, and the legislation pending in Congress to prevent the baby food manufacturers from pricing their products too high. Some of the other manufacturers were raising their prices but not too sharply.

Warren P. Bowman sat in his private office and watched his own image on the screen as he explained to the nation that he and his institute would guarantee that those who were new parents would not have to pay outrageous prices for the materials they would need.

There was an interview with Martin James and he said that he and his people would do their best to discover the reasons for the sudden glut of infants.

After a spate of commercials, the military people

announced that a constant search for aliens was being conducted everywhere in the world. A bald-headed general sat behind a massive desk and smiled at the camera as he explained that the Pentagon did not really accept the possibility of aliens being on earth, but just in case, hundreds of planes, piloted by trained personnel from the armed forces were criss-crossing the country, searching diligently, with highly sophisticated equipment, for any craft that might have become submerged on the planet.

Once he was gone from the screen, Warren lost interest. The news was mostly a rehash of what had previously been learned. He glanced at his watch and noticed that it was nearly six.

"Are we going to try to do any more today?"

He smiled and shook his head at Angie. She stood in front of his desk, her arms folded across her waist. She was wearing a dark brown dress and it was rumpled, wilted. She looked tired, ready to go home.

"Get rid of anyone that is waiting. Tell them to come back tomorrow or whenever you want us to deal with them. I'm going home, and I'd advise you to do the same."

Angie grinned. "I'll do it," she said.

She went out and he sat for a time behind his desk, smoking a cigarette. He went to a wall cabinet and poured himself a drink. He drank it down, neatly, quickly. He was in the bathroom, washing his hands when Angie's voice came onto the speaker.

"I'm leaving now," she said. "Good night."

He said good night and brushed his hair, what there was of it. He got his attache case from a closet, where Angie had put it. He closed up and went downstairs to the car.

The chauffeur was waiting to drive him home. He

settled back and held the black case between his feet, glancing out from time to time as the car rolled through the darkened streets. He stared for a while at the chauffeur's thick red neck and he wondered, idly, if the man had a girl friend, or a wife. He had never bothered to inquire. The man had been sent to him by an employment agency and he was a good driver. That was all that seemed to matter.

His mind shifted and the things that he had said to Orville came back to him. He didn't really want Orville to hurt Martin James and he was sure that Orville would not even consider such a crime. Orville was a nice little bunny rabbit and he would be helpful, cooperative, but he was not the type to injure anyone. He sighed as he realized that he had forgotten to have Angie send Orville a check. Oh, well, he could send it over in the morning.

The Rolls slid to a cushioned halt at the front of his mansion. The chauffeur opened the door for him and when he got out, the man drove off to the garages at the rear of the estate. Warren walked towards the door.

It opened for him a moment before he reached it. Gloria, his beautiful blonde butler, stood smiling, waiting for him to enter. She was a tall girl, spectacularly lovely in her tailored tuxedo. She was an excellent butler, handling the service problems in his home with great expertise and efficiency.

"Good evening, sir," she said. "Will you want dinner?"

He nodded. The girl reached for his attache case and he shook his head. "That's all right. I'll carry it. I'll be in the study. Please see to it that I am not disturbed."

"Yes, sir." She smiled, closed the door behind him and started for the kitchen. He walked through the marbled foyer and headed for his private study at the far end of the house.

He closed the heavy oak door behind him and locked it. The lights were on, automatically switched into illumination when he closed the door and locked it. He put the black case on top of the desk. While he was fixing a drink at the bar, the speaker came on and the housekeeper asked what he would like for his dinner. She said that she had some fine steaks. Would he like one for dinner?

He said yes and the speaker went dead again.

He sat down behind his desk, his drink close at hand. He got out his keys and used one of them to unlock the big black case. He opened it and began lifting out the piles of money it contained. It was packaged in small bills, each packet containing a thousand dollars. He checked the count and then closed the case again.

After a short time, he stood and went to stare at a large seascape that hung on the wall. His fingers reached behind the frame's edge and touched a hidden spring. The painting swung away from the wall and exposed the facade of a steel safe. He opened that and put the stacks of bills inside. There were many other stacks of bills in the big steel box. There was nearly a million dollars there. He would dispose of it properly soon. He stood for a time, gazing at the money, enjoying the experience. He closed the door finally and went back to the desk and his drink.

His dinner was a quiet, subdued experience. He sat at the head of the big dining room table while the servants placed his food in front of him. He dined in a splendor that was regal and when his meal was finished, he went back to the study and the work that was lying on the desk. It did seem to him that he was always able to accomplish more actual work in his study at home. When he mentioned it to Angie she pointed out that he was able to work undisturbed at his home. He could not manage that at the institute. So he had gotten into the habit of bringing the important work home with him.

He liked to sit at his desk in the privacy of his own home and go over the things he would have to do on the following day. He wished that he could persuade Amy Driscoll to come to his house. He would show her through it and he was sure that she would be properly admiring and aware of his status as a very successful businessman.

Perhaps she would be sufficiently impressed with the estate to think seriously of being its mistress. She might even have some suggestions for changes. And then she would want to marry him and take over the house and the grounds and the servants and his dream of happiness with his favorite person would be a reality. He realized that he was fantasizing and it annoyed him to face the probability that he would never have Amy for his own. He had certainly tried hard for her and he would keep on trying but he was just a little uncertain about the outcome.

The private line rang while he was working and he took the phone from the bottom desk drawer and answered it.

The voice on the other end was familiar, guarded.

"I'm very glad you called," Warren said. "I have some funds that I want you to handle for me. When can we arrange that?"

His caller was eager to do what was required of him.

"If you will meet me at midnight in the park on Twenty-fifth Street, I will take the money off your hands. I will wait for you in front of the statue of Prometheus. Where we usually meet."

The line went dead and Warren put the phone away. He stood up and went to the hidden safe. He got out twin suitcases and began stuffing them with money. When his task was finished, the big safe was empty.

He worked till very late. The house was quieted down when he picked up the expensive bags and carried them out to the garage. He opened the trunk of the Cadillac he usually drove himself and stowed the bags carefully. He covered them with a blanket that he kept in the trunk for beach parties or picnics. The darkness, beyond the cone of light that was provided by the garage light, was still, and he peered around, worried. No one seemed awake or near him. He closed the trunk lid, got in and drove the car out of the long driveway. He used his key to energize the big iron gates and drove out when they slid open. He heard the slight clang as they closed and locked behind him.

It was a long drive to the place that had been chosen as a meeting place. He lit a cigarette and played the car radio. He thought about Amy and Martin James and Orville Corby. He did not think about the man he was going to meet. He thought about the possibility of government supervision, the new taxation plan. That worried him. He had always had a free hand, he had run his large corporate entity as he chose. Once the government stepped in to monitor taxes and taxable procedures such as the institute's awards of the seal of approval and some of the other procedures the Triple I had engendered during its existence, it would end. The first thing the government people would do would be to audit the books and itemize things. He did not want that sort of thing to happen.

He entered the park and looked around him as he drove slowly towards the place of rendezvous. He knew the statue and he had met the same man there often in the past. He had not known that it was a statue of Prometheus. He didn't really care, anyway.

They were waiting for him.

There were three of them. The man who would take the money and two who would guard him and the suitcases. When he stopped his car and got out, they moved up to stand behind him. He lifted out the cases and the men took them from him. They went to the big black limousine and put the cases inside between the front seat and the back seat.

He stood and looked at the man who was taking charge of the money. He was a tall slender man with sharp angular features. With his long black coat and black hat he looked like an undertaker. He was not an undertaker, however.

He spoke softly. "Thank you, Mr. Bowman," he said. "Once again we meet in the dark of night to effect our purposes. It is nice to see you again."

Warren nodded. The somber-looking man held out his hand. They said good night and then Warren got back into his car. He drove back to his house slowly, thoughtfully. He turned the car radio on and listened to music as he drove. He did not want to think about the money that he had just turned over to others. He wanted to think about Amy and how wonderful life could be if he had her for his own for all time.

The radio's music stopped in the middle of a tune and there was a moment of silence. The voice of an excited announcer rattled loudly in the speaker and Warren listened in a state of stunned disbelief.

"We interrupt out regular program at this time," the announcer said, "to bring you a news bulletin. It has been announced that what appears to be a large space ship, submerged in a salt mine in Utah, has been discovered by teams of searchers in the area. All efforts to contact those who might be inside the vehicle from outer space have failed so far.

"Ladies and gentlemen, I just don't believe this," the man said, "but it is the bulletin we have been given. It had been well publicized that thousands of military technicians, using extremely new and sophisticated devices, have been combing the land everywhere, looking for some evidence of hidden space ships or whatever. One huge cigar-shaped cylinder was exposed during an earthquake in a small community in northern California, but now we are told that hundreds of such cylinders have been located buried in the earth all over the world.

"The searchers in Utah are convinced that what they have located is indeed a space ship, hidden, well concealed, and occupied. It is said the machinery and life signs have been detected and attempts to contact those in the space ship will begin at daylight.

"At this time, the area has been cordoned off and ringed with armed military personnel. General Amos Cramer, head of the military in the sector, has asked that all people stay away from the site."

A statement from the general was inserted then. "Until we know what we've found, until we know whether thse people, and there are people down there, we know, are friendly or hostile, we want to avoid risking any lives. The public will be kept informed as the search progresses."

"Well, that seems to be it, ladies and gentlemen," the announcer continued. "We return you now to our program of music and we will interrupt to bring you bulletins as they are received."

The music came back on the radio and Warren tried to digest what had been broadcast. He didn't really believe that they had found a buried space ship. Some kids, maybe, with a tin hut that they had put up deep in a salt mine. That he could believe. The other was pure, arrant nonsense.

He was still thinking about it as he put the car away and let himself into the house. He settled down in his study for a drink and a smoke and a bit of television. If something had been found it would be on the tube. And it was. Each channel was busy with the news. One station apologized for not being able to bring its viewers a picture of the site and what was taking place there.

An announcer, doing a voice-over off screen, said, "This is the type of terrain the buried space ship is in, but we were not allowed over the area. Our news plane was told to get out of the area and stay out or risk being shot down, so we bring you only what we can at the moment. We have been assured by General Amos Cramer that the news media will be kept up to date as details develop."

The scene shifted to an in-studio interview with one of the science-fiction writers, an incredible bore who was always on the TV tube, trying with pathetic determination for some respect as a scholar or a prophet. Warren switched to another channel. There was another science-fiction writer holding forth on that channel, too, trying to decide if there really could be visitors from outer space in the Utah salt mine. The metal detectors had exposed the hiding place and some of the other highly complex equipment had established that there were living beings below the earth's surface at the site.

He tried another channel and found several well-known newscasters sitting around a table, trying to decide if they were dealing with the first invasion of Earth by foreign beings or hoax. Elwood Grimes, one of the most respected newsmen, was inclined to suspect a hoax. He supposed that the whole world was in a state that bordered upon hysteria, mainly because of the startling changes that had taken place within Earth's females, the glut of babies that could easily starve in a world unprepared for their arrival, and the general attitude of fantasy that had captivated the people of Earth in the recent past.

Warren kept changing channels, expecting to

learn new information at each step, but there was nothing new. He switched back to the science-fiction writer and listened to the man's asininities for a time. He was not too surprised when his telephone began to ring. He was glad of the interruption.

It was Orville Corby and he was excited. "You know about the buried space ship?" he asked.

"I'm watching television," Warren said. "I'm not sure that I can accept the idea of a space ship and beings from another planet. I will just wait and see."

"I tried to call you earlier, Warren," Orville said.

"I was out. I had an errand to run. What did you want?"

"I didn't get any money, Warren. You promised I would have it today and I didn't get it."

Warren sighed. He was watching the TV screen, only partially engaged with Orville.

"I'll have Angie make it out in the morning and give it to you. Why don't you come in and see me bright and early and I'll personally see to it that you are paid. What do the computers say about what's going on now, Orville? You've been down to the institute, haven't you?"

"No. I have a monitor here. I checked, but there is nothing new on the lines. I asked for an analytical prediction and the machines say that the possibility of space aliens and a buried space ship is possible. Extremely likely. The presence of aliens is the only explanation the computers will now accept for the things that have been happening here for the last six months."

Warren said, "I was afraid of that. What do we do now, Orville?"

"We wait, I guess. See you in the morning."

Warren said good night. He put the phone away and sat back to watch the TV screen and sip his drink.

He glanced at his watch and got a shock. It was a little after three in the morning. Orville was up late. He suspected that most of the world would be wide awake now.

And decidedly alarmed.

He was trembling. He continued to watch the TV set and as the bulletins piled up he began to believe in the space ship. And in its peoples, too.

"It has been revealed," one announcer reported, "that the exact location of the alien space ship was practically pinpointed by the physicists at the Institute of Applied Logic. Using highly sophisticated equipment in a drone plane, Doctor David Trumbull and his wife, Mrs. Lily Trumbull, selected the rugged terrain of Utah and its salt mines as a possible hiding place for a space ship. Constant searching has finally paid off and the aliens have been located. Now, contact is being attempted."

Warren finally went off to his bed. He felt slightly ill.

CHAPTER SIX

The lights were blinding him and Martin closed his eyes against their glare. It didn't seem to help. He could feel prickling, burning sensations everywhere in his body and he was conscious of a delicious lassitude, a warm, enervating weariness that wrapped his entire being into a cocoon of extreme comfort.

Someone was slapping his face and it hurt. His brain stirred, began to function. He opened his eyes again and the stark white of the walls and the ceiling were not what he might have expected. Then he remembered and he supposed that he and Nora and the major had survived the trip in the space capsule and they were now reviving him.

A pretty brunette in the white uniform of a nurse came close to his bed. She stood, looking down at him.

She smiled. "How do you feel, Mister James?"

He sat up. He felt fit, alert, eager to get out of the bed.

"I'm fine," he said. "How are Nora and the major?"

The nurse smiled down at him. "They are all right, too. But I'd better not talk to you any more. There are important people waiting to see you as soon as you are recovered. I'll tell them you are awake."

She poured him a cup of hot coffee and he picked it up and sipped it. It tasted just like coffee that he had been used to on Earth. The nurse went out and a moment later he was surprised to see Randy Mapes walk in. The senator was smiling at him, obviously not at all concerned about the way things were.

"He's probably one of them," he thought. Mapes was walking toward him, glad to see him alive and well. He had that look.

"You gave us a very real scare there for a while, Marty," the senator said. "They almost got you away from us. You were very lucky. Very lucky."

He stared at Randy Mapes. He had no idea what the man was talking about. He took another sip of the hot coffee hoping that it would stir his brain to its usual efficiency. The door opened again and the major came into the room. He was smiling.

"How do you feel, Mr. James?" he asked.

Martin nodded, indicating that he was fine. He was about to ask where they were and how long they had been frozen when the major said, "We were very lucky, Mr. James. The boys working outside noticed the frost forming on the hull and when it started humming, lifting itself up off the ground, one of the boys on a bulldozer smashed the door in with his big blade. That ended our little trip right then and there. They found us nearly frozen and rushed us to the hospital. You took a little longer to snap back. Your associate is downstairs in the coffee shop. She'll be along shortly, I'm sure."

Martin began to laugh and Randy Mapes stared at him worriedly.

"I thought we were on another planet." he said. "I really thought they had us."

Randy Mapes shook his head. "You've been here most of the day. But, in the meanwhile, we have our technicians going over that hull. The people who designed it are fiendishly clever. Too, I can tell you, in privacy, that there have been other such hulls located all over the world. And they are all alike. Obviously, they are incubators intended to travel into outer space. Perhaps the machines have been right all along. What do you think?"

Martin sipped some more coffee. He lit a cigarette that he took from the package that was on the bedside table.

"I think we are getting closer to the truth now. There are certain facts that seem to be related. For instance, our computer terminals were wrecked but no one was hurt. We found a bomb aboard our plane but there was time to fly out to sea and jettison the bomb. Again, no one was hurt. Then when we went aboard the space ship or whatever it is, we were saved from death or a bad experience, so I'm beginning to wonder what is really going on. Obviously, they don't want to kill anyone. As yet."

Randy Mapes sat down in the chair beside the bed. He was wearing a dark black suit and it was rumpled. His tie was slightly askew and his shirt was soiled.

"Once I heard about the bomb and then the freezing hull out there, I got a plane and came out here to see for myself. I spent a lot of time going over that space ship. We don't know yet how things work aboard the craft but it is obviously very cleverly constructed."

The major was standing beside the window looking out into the night. He turned to look at Martin. "From what they've told me, as soon as the door was smashed in and the pressure became altered everything simply stopped and the hull settled back to earth again. The engineers that have been going over it think they may have to take the vehicle apart in order to find out how it functions."

Randy Mapes wanted to say things. He was sure that he had put Mary and Nora in a position where they were vulnerable and susceptible to danger and perhaps death.

"It was very foolish of me to release the news that you and your institute and its associates had been retained by the government. I'm sure that the people we are seeking, if they are people, are monitoring our television and know everything that we have broadcast, so far. So, they know about you and your computers and they are trying to kill you in order to protect themselves. That's the way it appears. You'd better be very careful."

Before he could answer, a white-coated young man with dangling stethoscope, came in and began checking Martin over. He was quite thorough. When he finished, he stood back and looked at Martin with a solemn expression on his young face.

"You are perfectly all right," he said. "The lab tests that we ran on you are all okay and I see no reason why you can't get out of bed."

Martin grinned. He swung his legs out of the bed

and put them on the floor. He stood and found that all of his strength had returned. He flexed his fingers and the tingling sensation had left them. The doctor opened the closet door beside the bed and handed his clothes to him. He began getting dressed.

Nora arrived while he was brushing his hair. She was smoking a ciagrette and clutching her purse against her chest.

"Close," she said. "Someone doesn't like us, I guess."

Randy Mapes stood and gazed at them, his lips pursed into an expression of great concentration.

"Now what?" he said.

Martin said, "We are going to get aboard that flying computer-processing center and go home. We'd better check on any latest developments. We've done all that we can here."

Randy Mapes said, "I'd like to hitch a ride, if I may? I think I should get back to Washington."

Martin said, "You are welcome to come along with us. Once we get aboard our ship we can check with our engineers and be brought up to date right away."

Nora yawned. It startled her and she grinned at him. "I am going to try for some sleep. Freezing, or nearly doing it, seems to tire me."

The major was helpful in facilitating their departure from the hospital. He rode with them in the closed military vehicle that was waiting for them.

"We have not released any information about your experiences here," he said. "I have orders that require me to keep any information I may become privy to a secret. Top secret."

Randy Mapes pushed his back tightly against the cushions of the car. He got out cigars and offered them to the major and Martin. The major took one. They lit up, Randy Mapes held the cigar between fingers, sniffing at the aromatic fragrance that was wavering from its tip. He turned to look at Martin.

"During the past week, there have been several such cylinders located in various parts of the world. But they were immediately guarded by the military and their existence was kept secret. Even from you and me. I think that was wrong and I will look into it. I may not get anywhere," he added, "but I will sure try."

The military car took them to a helicopter pad and they said good-bye to the major and got aboard for the short flight back to the jumbo jet.

It was still sitting where they had left it, a virtual army ringing it. Someone had ordered cannon, too. There were four howitzer-mounted tanks sitting in a four-cornered pattern guarding the huge plane. A thoughtful commander sent a jeep to carry them to the big plane and they went aboard with the general in charge. He accepted their thanks and then went back to his troops. The plane's great engines began whining, squealing, then as they began to warm up, several trucks carried the troops off.

The big plane began to move slowly, ponderously, and they could feel the effects of the uneven terrain they were crossing.

"Attention, all aboard," the captain's voice said in the speakers, "we are approaching takeoff. Lock all seats into place and fasten seat belts."

Nora and Randy Mapes were already settled in. He touched the button that locked his chair, then he put the seat belt on and tightened it. The plane was moving faster, trundling along on the approach strip. The plane's motion smoothed out and he knew that they were on the runway. The roar of the jets was deafening for a moment and then they were moving, sliding, bumping. Suddenly they were airborne and the incredible smoothness of flight was, momentarily, intensely pleasant.

"We are airborne, folks," the captain said.

Martin loosened the seat belt. He got up and waited for Nora and Randy Mapes.

"We can go into the terminal room now and find out what is going on in the outside world."

He glanced at his watch and saw that it was a little after ten at night. That meant it was a little after midnight on the East Coast. A feeling of great weariness set in and he decided that he would turn in for a nap after he checked the computer banks and read the printouts.

Nora and the senator went along with him. The plane was streaking through the night sky and the people who were aboard worked at their usual tasks. Their work went on whether the computers were on land or in the air. He wondered if some of them ever noticed the difference.

They stood for a time in front of one of the TV screens that was showing the printouts in twenty-second frames. There was a monotonous repetitiveness about the words that leapt and danced on the screen. The same bulletins or new printouts were being show on computers and receiving machines all around the world. The screen dealt with the location of the huge metal cylinder and its examination by experts but nothing was mentioned about their brush with death.

Randy Mapes said, "Some of the new information has been labelled top secret. That's why it doesn't show up on the computers. It has to be that way. We are trying to avoid panic."

Another complex of computers was revealing the prices of stock everywhere in the world, and, in spite of the fact that the stock markets were closed, the machines were printing out the day's closing prices, because everything was being affected by the many births that were taking place.

Since the inception of the new gestation term and

115

the onset of the many births, every phase of the economy had been touched. Housing, medicine, clothing, hospitalization, medicine in all of its branches, stocks, and everything else, presumably. Martin stood with Nora and Randy, watching as the notations and the figures changed on the multiple screens in front of them.

A feeling of weariness swept over him and he glanced at his watch.

"I think I'll turn in and try to get some rest," he said.

Nora looked at him with a solemn face.

"I didn't really get to do any of the things I hoped to do. I was going to get some scrapings from inside that thing to take back for analysis, and I wanted some scrapings from the hull, too. Instead, I seem to have come along for the ride."

"It was almost quite a ride," he said. "Let's get some rest."

They left the computer room and ran into some of the girls who were handling the catering and the hostessing aboard. Most of the women were busy with the working personnel, but Lola Madison, a tall, slender blonde who had worked for a major airline and wanted to make more money, took over and guided Nora and Randy Mapes to bedrooms that would offer them a chance for rest. Martin said good night and went off to the private suite he used.

He used the small shower and then slid between the cool sheets. He could hear the whistling roar of the engines, but it was an undertone, a sound that was comforting, somehow.

He stretched out in the darkness and tried to sleep but his mind was busy with the events that had nearly killed him. It did seem that some alien presence was trying to destroy him.

Martin wondered about aliens. Could it be possible that there were invaders? He didn't know but he supposed that he would find out. And maybe they could put a stop to the baby boom. A world that had been filled with diversified interests and many ambitions was now totally interested in infants and the problems that their entrance into the world brought on.

There were foundling homes springing up all around the world, homes where unwanted children could grow like regimented little cabbages and Warren P. Bowman seemed not to care for those children. The hospitals were funneling them into the orphanages, into the children's hospitals that cared for those who had defects. There were very few of those, but they were the ones that no one seemed to want. Many parents, faced with the economic impossibility of raising many children, simply gave them up to the homes. At first, there were many couples who wanted to adopt children but then babies became as numerous as sand pebbles and the procedures of adoption became streamlined and simplified, finally degenerating into a system that would place a child in the arms of anyone who would take it. And most important, could the earth supply food and water for all these people?

He was still thinking about the problems that so many babies were forcing upon the world when he fell asleep.

He liked to sleep on a plane. There was something soporific about being in flight. It was like being in a giant cradle and the slight motion would induce deep sleep. He was dreaming, he knew. He was with a very lovely young girl. She had long golden hair and beautiful eyes. Her mouth was red and sweet and exceedingly lovely. Especially when she smiled and she seemed to smile a lot. She was with him in a deep green meadow and they were holding hands and she was wearing a trim white blouse, a dark

117

blue skirt and sandals. She sat down and there was a fence for them to sit on and she was trying to explain things to him.

"Thenna hates you. I don't know why. And it is very unusual for us to hate. We are not emotional. But I do like you and Thenna knows it. He is behaving just like a very jealous earthling. He put the bomb into your auto but I made sure that you did not use your car. And, when he put the explosives in your plane, I made certain that you had plenty of time to get rid of it. Thenna tried to send you back to Rombella in the shuttle ship but I put a thought into the head of the young man driving that big thing and he pushed the door open.

"I am very sorry that Thenna does not like you but I will try to make sure that he does not really hurt you. He is already in difficulties now. Omborg knows all about what he has been doing and he is going to be punished."

"I'm so glad that you are with me," Marty said. "What is your name?"

The girl's smile highlighted her beautiful face the way a sunbeam brightens a somber day. "I am Olva. Just Olva. I am very sorry we had to destroy your machines, but we cannot let your people discover us as yet. We are helpless at the moment. There is hope that we will become friends with your people."

Her beautiful face was close to his own. He was gazing into her eyes, drowning in the softness, the luminescence that he found there. She leaned close and he kissed her, their lips brushing against each other in a friendly, curious buss.

"I like you, Martin James," she said. "I like you very much. I would like to have you for my friend. Can we ever be friends?"

He stared into her eyes and he felt a gentle warmth flooding his breasts. The urge to have her for a friend was suddenly overwhelming. She reached out to place her warm palm against his cheek and then she was slapping his cheek, hurting him. He was shocked, amazed.

He woke and found Nora in his room. The lights were on and she was dressed. She was sitting on the edge of his bed, shaking him, trying to awaken him. He sat up and stared at her.

He shook his head, trying to clear it.

"I was dreaming," he said.

She nodded, her eyes twinkling at him. "What were you dreaming about?"

He tried to remember and could not. "What time is it?"

"It's three o'clock in the morning back East. I don't know where we are right now so I don't know what the time is here but that is not important. Lily and David are wide awake and Lily is on the phone. She wants to talk to you and she says it is important enough to wake you."

He found his cigarettes and got one lit. He sucked smoke into his lungs and then exhaled, slowly, savoring the taste of the smoke. He reached out and flicked a switch on a small wall panel.

"Let's hear what she wants," he said. With the key open, he said, "Hi, Lily. This is Marty."

"Oh, Marty," Lily said, "I'm so glad that I was able to reach you. Is it all right to talk?"

He glanced at Nora. She nodded, which meant that she had accepted the call on one of the very private lines.

"Go ahead, Lily. What's up? How come you are out of bed at this hour?"

Lily said, "David is out of bed, too. We are at your house, using the equipment there. We seem to have located our aliens, Marty. David and I have been very busy since you and Nora went off to look at that hull. We suggested to the Pentagon that they begin using Geiger counters in their low-flying helicopters, and heat-seeking gear, too. They've been using metal-seeking equipment but it seems that the metals the other people are using are unfamiliar to our engineers and standard mechanisms just won't work. The point is, I think we have located an alien space ship buried deep in a salt mine in Utah."

He was silent a moment while he tried to accept what she had said. "You realize what you are saying?"

Lily was quite sure. "We've known about it for some hours now, and we were hoping to keep it secret until you could get home and take over, but someone at the site leaked the information to the news people and they are getting ready to release it as soon as they can get official clearance. In the meanwhile, the communications experts are making every effort to establish some sort of communications. So far there has been no response. David thought we should contact you in flight. You might want to go directly to the site in Utah."

"Yes. We will. I'll have to talk to the pilots and see what they can do about getting us there."

"Keep in touch," Lily said.

Nora put her fingertip on the key and shut the phone off. She looked at him for a time, wondering, uncertain as to whether she should accept what Lily said as fact.

"I'll meet you in the galley," she said. "We should eat while we have the chance."

He nodded. She went out and he got out of bed and into his clothing. He brushed his teeth and shaved, quickly, deftly, with the electric razor. He felt quite fit, thoroughly recovered from the near-fatal experience he had had with frost.

Just before he left the cabin he pressed the button that energized the direct line he had to the pilots.

"Bernie," he said to the chief pilot, "how about meeting me in the galley? Right now."

"Okay," the man said.

Nora had a table for them in the main dining room. There were many people in the vast room, some having a cup of coffee before going to bed, some having it before going on duty. He sat down in the booth with Nora and a waitress came over to get his order. A moment later, Bernie Graham, the chief pilot, slid into the booth with them. He was a nice-looking man, barely into his thirties. He liked Nora and she stifled a smile as he stared at her with his usual adoring look. He turned to look at Martin and then he was all business.

"You want something?" he said.

"They think that there is a space ship buried in a salt mine in Utah. What are the chances of you landing this thing at the site?"

"If they'll give us an exact location and keep the area we land in clear, we can set down without much difficulty."

Martin said, "How?"

Bernie sneaked a glance at Nora and she tilted her head to gaze at him and smile.

"Once we are over the landing area we can drop down to a thousand feet and then raise the rotor blades. That will turn this ship into a helicopter. We can set down easily then in a very small space. That the way you want it?"

"That's probably the way it will have to be."

Bernie Graham was about to go back to the main control room when someone switched on the television and the giant, wallsized screen filled up, first with a science-fiction writer who always seemed to get himself on the TV screen when anything of unusual importance occurred. He was eager to insist that the reports of alien beings found in a salt mine would turn out to be a hoax. Life on other planets just was not a possibility. And, if life could not exist on other planets, no one from outer space could invade Earth.

The chief switched channels and they watched a network news show cover the extending food riots and the hoarding of water in almost all major cities throughout the world. Hysteria was added to panic as the news of the alien beings filtered through to the furthest reaches of the Earth. Commentators tried to establish fact from fiction, and discount the rumors that were racing around the world with the speed of sound.

"It is very late back East," Nora remarked, "but it would seem that everybody is awake."

"Where are we right now?" Martin asked.

Bernie glanced at his watch. "We are close to New York by now. Probably stacked over the airport." He pulled a two-way radio out of his jacket pocket. "Bernie here," he said. "Give me a fix, will you, Don?"

"We're home, Pappy," Don Borron said. "We are waiting for clearance and landing instructions."

"Cancel," Martin said. "Let's turn this thing around and head back to Utah. Try for a fix on the salt mine where all the activity is, and see if we can land in the area."

Bernie stood up. He glanced at Nora again and then gave his full attention to Martin. "This will take some doing," he said. "I have to ask for permission to cancel our request for landing, then we have to file a new destination and get permission and instructions about leaving the stack."

"If you need muscle," Martin said, "we have Senator Randy Mapes aboard. He's sleeping, but we can wake him up if we need some real power."

Martin finished his coffee. He was watching the TV screen and it occurred to him that nothing new was being shown. He glanced at Bernie and the pilot waved as he headed back to his job.

"You'd better send someone in and wake up Randy. If this information turns out to be true, he will never forgive us if he misses any of it. He will want to be aware of what is going on every minute."

"I'll send a steward in with some coffee for him," Nora said. She flagged their waitress and Nora asked to have someone wake the senator and bring him some coffee. "Ask him to meet us in the conference room when he can."

The girl nodded and went off. They finished their coffee and stood, ready for the conference room, when Bernie piped them into his conversation with the control tower at New York.

"IAL Number One calling tower," he said. "Requesting to cancel landing and asking to change destination."

"Tower to IAL One," the traffic controller said, "permission denied. Proceed to land as planned. You have been assigned altitude and you will be brought in when possible."

Bernie got a little nasty at that point. "We are leaving here," he said. "You give us clearance or we fly out on visible and radar. Make up your mind."

The controller was nasty, too. "You try to move and we'll send up a military plane to shoot you down. All civilian units have been grounded as of now."

"You better not get hardnosed with us, buddy," Bernie said. "We have Senator Randolph Mapes aboard and Martin James, too. This is Martin James' plane. You want to try having us shot down?"

"We will want to talk with Senator Mapes," the tower man said. He sounded sullen. "General Crosley Fields is commanding this sector at present and there is talk of declaring martial law here. People are jamming the streets trying to find out what's going on. The TV doesn't tell 'em much. We only know that we have been told that all nonmilitary aircraft are to be grounded until further orders."

"You get the general to the radio, Dad," Bernie said. "He can talk things over with my boss and the senator. Maybe we can find out who is running the country."

"Will do," the towerman said. He sighed. "All I need to know is who's running the airport. I'll ask the general to talk to your people. You hold position until he does it."

"Sure," Bernie said. "We got time."

Bernie flipped his switch and the radio noise went away.

He left the galley with Nora and they found that the TV screens in the conference room were alive with news people and science-fiction writers and some people were saying that it was possible that the planet Earth had been invaded, some said it was nonsense. While they were getting settled in front of the panels and the screens, their waitress from the galley brought in a steaming pot of coffee. She put it down on the shelf in front of them.

"The senator said to tell you that he would join you here as soon as he was washed and brushed his teeth. The steward told him what has been going on. I mean about finding the buried space ship and all."

Martin laughed. "He probably didn't believe a word of it."

The waitress smiled. "I don't either," she said.

Martin sat back and looked at the panels in front of him. They looked like something out of a science-fiction movie with the varied colored lights running and flowing and shifting in colorful patterns that actually had meaning for the receiving machines. The TV screens were still cluttered with armchair experts and an occasional newscaster, trying to bring everyone up to date with information that was a rehash of what had been broadcast on one of the other channels.

Randy Mapes walked in and sat down. He poured himself a cup of coffee and looked at the screen.

"This stuff for real?" he said.

Martin nodded. He brought the senator up to date in a hurry. Including the hassle with the tower man.

"I agree that we should get out of here and set down close to that space ship," Randy Mapes said. "I guess I'd better talk to that general. How do we manage that?"

Martin reached out and flipped the switch on the videophone. He said, "Calling tower, come in, tower."

"Tower here," the controller said. Martin made some adjustments and the man's face came onto the video screen of the phone.

"Senator Randy Mapes wants to talk to the commanding officer for the area. What did you say his name was?"

A new face, topped by the ornate hat of a general came onto the screen. "General Crosley Fields here," he said. "What's the trouble here? I'm a busy man. A very busy man."

Martin smiled at Randy Mapes. "He's a very busy man. You'd better talk to him."

Mapes sat in the chair in front of the transmitter screen. "General," he said, "we want to get away from here and go out to where the space ship is said to be buried. Do we need to be cleared by you?"

"This is really Senator Randolph Mapes? Yes, I see that it is. You will be given clearance immediately, sir. We are grounding all other aircraft for the time being. Perhaps I can bring you up to date. You have decoding equipment aboard?"

The senator looked at Martin. He nodded. The general began talking and it was pure gibberish. A coding scrambler was at work in both receiver and transmitter. When the general was finished with what he was saying, he began talking sensibly again.

"After you have decoded the message, you will see that it is imperative for you to get out there. In the meanwhile, have your pilot talk to the controller and he will be given new instructions so that your plane can leave."

The general said good-bye and the screen went white again. Martin yawned. He looked at his watch. It was nearly five in the morning. When he drew the curtain of one of the ports and looked out it was nearly daylight.

He poured himself some fresh coffee and he lit a cigarette. They felt the plane lurch and he knew that Bernie was turning it around, heading back out west.

A page brought them the decoded message in a sealed envelope. It had been sealed by the decoder. Martin open it as Randy Mapes looked over his shoulder.

"The space ship is real and we have made contact with the people inside. They admit that they are from another planet and they are willing to talk to a representative. But, they will talk with just one person. They seem to know all about him.

"They want to talk with Martin James."

CHAPTER SEVEN

They tried to find out more about the aliens while the plane was on its way to Utah. The military was setting up a command post very close to the site where the space ship was said to be. From the moment of discovery, the people who manned the contact and communications equipment began a massive effort to get in touch with the living beings who were aboard the buried space ship. They tried all sorts of sophisticated methodology. After hours of no response, the military linguists and telecommunications experts were about ready to give up when their speakers suddenly crackled with the carrier wave noises of a response.

"We are able to comprehend and speak in your language," a well-modulated voice said. "We wish to talk to one of you. We would be glad to welcome Mister Martin James, if he will come to see us. While you are arranging this, we would ask that an area one square mile in size be cleared. We intend to set up a force field so that we may move onto your planet's surface. We will wait for one hour and then move ahead with our preparations.

"We want to emphasize that it is not our intentions to hurt or damage anyone. Therefore, if you will do as we ask, we can begin our visit to Earth on a friendly basis."

The speakers went dead again and the technicians gaped at each other, astounded, not really believing that an extraterrestrial being had actually spoken to them.

The sound recordist played the tape back and they listened. A sergeant looked at the clock in the face of the machines they were using and he said, "We'd better talk to the brass. We have got a lot to do if we are going to clear a square mile. This place is jammed with people now."

Martin James and Nora sat with Randy Mapes and listened to the highly classified report from the site. There were closed-circuit pictures of the devastation and confusion that took place when the hour of space people wanted used for clearing was gone and the top brass refused to accede to their wishes.

A slender finial shot up out of the earth after the time period was at an end. It glowed brightly then it began to create an ever-widening force field. When the force field encountered matter in its way, it pushed and trucks and jeeps and tanks and aircraft turned over and slid on the ground, moving away from the edges of the force field. People, aware of the inexorable force that was clearing the area, fled, on foot, in vehicles. What the military refused to do, the space people accomplished with effortless ease. The movement of the outer rim of the force field was slow, no one was injured, but the pictures that a hovering military helicopter took showed the hasty exodus that was finally achieved.

Daylight had come at the site and the brilliant Utah sun made everything that took place remarkably visible. The cameras were fixed upon the finial and the area that surrounded it.

It looked like a hundred bulldozers, invisible, invincible, were moving the materials back that cluttered the terrain, clearing a vast area. And then, when the litter of overturned vehicles and equipment trucks, was removed, the ground began to shiver and shake.

Randy Mapes was smoking a cigarette and sipping a cup of coffee as he watched the huge TV screens and the activity taking place. Everyone not on duty in the plane was watching, too, and when Martin noticed them, he saw that each had a look of fear.

"I wonder why they want to talk to you," Randy Mapes said.

"We'll know pretty soon," Martin replied.

Nora looked at him, worriedly. "Aren't you scared?"

He nodded. "Of course. But they had plenty of chances to kill us and they didn't do it. So, I will worry when I have to worry."

A loud, concerted gasp escaped the people in the room and Martin turned back to watch the screen. A huge space ship was slowly rising up out of a hole that closed in below it again. Then it hovered while four legs protruded from its bottom. It was a saucer-shaped vehicle but it was a thousand feet in diameter, presumably, and the dome was at least ten stories high. It was a gleaming, white metal ship and as he stared at it, Martin was impressed by its simple beauty. There was a high, keening sound as the ship settled down onto its legs and then there was silence as the machinery shut off and the great ship sat, waiting, silent, ominous.

The cameras panned the area and they watched tents going up, huge military vehicles wheeling into position to form a massive square, ringing the space vehicle.

They were virtually enthralled by what they were watching and when their own speaker system erupted into sound, Martin jumped.

Bernie Graham announced that they were over the site and they would move down to a lower altitude and then land. Buckle up, everybody.

They sat in their chairs and waited. When the rotor blades were energized and lifted from their nests in the plane's crown, it felt as if they were suspended in a huge balloon. The jet plane floated lazily down to the ground and they felt the slight shock when the wheels touched down.

When the plane was still, Martin and Randy were ready to disembark. Nora looked at Martin, head tilted in questioning attitude.

"We would very much like you to visit us, too, Miss Nora Corwin." A voice raced through her brain. "We wish to discuss some problems we have encountered and the matter may very well be your province. Do come along, please."

It was the same voice that they had heard on the TV screen. Nora wore a startled look. "They read minds, too, obviously," she said. The others had also felt the spoken words.

Martin smiled grimly. "So come along."

They went forward to stand on the plane's

elevator platform. Martin touched a button and they were lowered to the ground, probably sixty feet below them.

There were hordes of people in uniform all around them and a general with five shining stars for insignia, stepped forward to offer his hand to Senator Mapes.

"This is General Tidy Metz," the senator said to Martin and Nora. He is in charge of West Coast operations."

The general shook hands with them. He was as friendly, as eager to please, as a puppy.

"They want to talk to you, Mister James," he said. "If you like, we will give you an escort right up to the entrance of their force field. No one can go any farther."

A startled look came over the face of Senator Mapes.

"Someone just spoke to me. I was invited to accompany you."

The voice spoke to Martin, too. "That's right, Mister James. We would be glad to welcome you and your pretty associate and the senator. If you will proceed to the edge of the cleared area, you will be permitted to pass through the force field. We will await you inside."

Nora said, "Maybe they intend to ambush us."

The voice spoke in their minds again. "We mean no harm. we need your help. We will explain when you come aboard."

"Oh, Great and Invisible One," Nora said, "who are you? How will we know that you are the one wo spoke to us?"

"I am Omborg, the Number One Superior. I will welcome you aboard and introduce you to the others. We are hoping for friendship. And, of course, some assistance with our difficulties."

Martin glanced at Randy Mapes. The senator

shrugged. "I'm sure that these people know that any attempt at hostile activity will bring forth horrible and devastating repercussions."

Omborg answered in the minds of each of them. "We assume that you are prepared to order hostility, but that won't be necessary. It would not be wise to do so. Your most awesome weapon, we believe, is the hydrogen bomb. Such a device would not damage our force field or penetrate it. The energy from the explosion would simply be stored and absorbed into our energy banks. Do come along and we will talk face to face, and, hopefully, more intelligently."

General Tidy Metz joined them as they began walking towards the space ship. It rested, glowing slightly with a soft luminescence that seemed to heighten its beauty. Martin found that he was holding Nora's hand as they walked and he wondered when he had done that. Randy Mapes walked behind them. The five-star general was beside him. The general seemed to think that he was going to go aboard the space ship, too. Martin did not say anything, but he did wonder if the space people would want a representative of the military along for the initial interview.

They reached the edge of the force field and paused. Martin noted the columns of uniformed soldiers that were behind them, accompanying them. He looked at the general and the man's smug smile annoyed him.

The voice of Omborg boomed and they listened as he spoke.

"We will confine our first interview to a talk with Mister Martin James, his associate, Miss Nora Corwin, and Senator Randy Mapes. If you three will approach the force field, one at a time, you will pass through the field without noticing its existence."

Nora smiled at Martin and stepped forward. She walked toward the space ship. Randy Mapes followed her. Martin followed the senator. He said good-bye to the general for the time being and caught up with Nora and the senator.

Once they were inside the force field, a small mechanical cart came for them. There was no one in the cart. They sat on the seats and the cart turned and moved towards the space ship. The distance was probably a half mile and the ride was swift and smooth.

Nora said, "I wonder if we will be given a ride back again."

No one answered her. When the cart halted beneath the space ship's belly, a stairway moved down slowly and they began their climb. They were standing on the stairway's treads when the steps began moving upwards again, relieving them of the need to walk. They held onto the railings and faced each other, their smiles not at all sturdy.

The stairway flattened out its steps slowly, almost imperceptibly as it became a part of the flooring. There were three impossibly beautiful young girls in shorts and halters, waiting with sparkling smiles, to usher them into a large room. They stepped onto a moving belt that carried them to the room where many people sat within a large triangular set of tables and three bearded men sat at the corner of each point of the triangle. One point of the triangle faced a cluster of chairs, obviously arranged for visitors. The man seated in that chair looked to be forty, perhaps. He had the slender body of a tall man and the gentie, intelligent eyes of the scholar.

He waved them into seats. "I am Omborg," he said. "I am Supervisor Number One. Kaffal, on your left, is Supervisor Number Two. Rissel, on your right is Supervisor Number Three."

Martin bowed. Randy Mapes and Nora bowed, too. Omborg told them, without speaking, to sit down. He smiled and looked very much like a vice president in somebody's insurance company.

"We are very pleased to meet you, Mister Martin James. Speaking for all of us, I would like to say that we are very sorry that you have been menaced and your machines have been damaged because of us. We intended no harm to anyone."

A beautiful brunette, seated just behind Omborg, spoke up.

"We must tell you that a very jealous young man was easily persuaded to do you harm by Kaspin, our chief of wardens. Kaspin is a vicious man, jealous of you and your accomplishments. He wants you destroyed. I am Lichela, Chief Warden of the Females. The young lady who accompanied Thenna, the jealous young man, was told to see to it that no harm came to you. I'm glad that she was able to carry out her assignment."

A slender young girl, incredibly blonde and lovely, with large, luminous eyes, smiled at him and Martin had the vague notion that he had seen her before.

"You people are responsible for the baby glut?" Randy Mapes said.

Omborg spoke aloud. "Yes," he said. "We admit that it is an experiment that got out of hand. But it was something that we felt we had to do."

"You wanted babies?" Randy Mapes just didn't seem to understand. He sat in his chair, obviously impressed by the people within the triangle.

Omborg said, "We left a planet that was a sterile hulk in the universe. Our biologists worked very hard to perfect a cure for our problems and when they had achieved their purposes, it was much too late for their miracles to do us any good at home. We love the planet that we came from, much as you

Earth people do yours, I'm sure.

"Our biologists assured us that the processes of human gestation that they had worked out could be made to work on the planet Earth and we could reap a grand harvest of infants. It was our plan to send the infants back to our planets and begin our culture all over again."

Nora was outraged. "You wanted to use the females of Earth as brood mares and then steal their children from them. That's awful. Really awful."

Omborg smiled at her but it was a contrived grimace really, not at all attractive.

"We did not think of our task in that way. It is perfectly possible for us to take the infant from its mother, much as you do with kittens and puppy dogs. We can erase all memory of childbirth or having a child with a simple wave of our hand. It was and is as simple as that."

"But something went wrong," Martin said. "That's why you allowed us to discover your presence. That's why we are here. You need our help. What do you want?"

Omborg's manufactured smile showed again. It was very like the grin on the dog's face when he has been caught sucking eggs.

"Our shuttle ships, designed to carry the infants safely back to our planet, must be guided through the time and space continuum by our computers. But, in your heavily polluted atmosphere, our computers are not dependable or accurate. They must be corrected, and recalibrated so that they will function as they must. That is why we need your help."

Martin said, "Your vandals destroyed our machines so we can't help you."

One of the other Superiors spoke up. He had been identified as Kaffal, the number two man. He said, "That was not something that we ordered. A bitter young man, jealous because his female companion found you attractive, likable, became enraged and did the damage you mention. We will be glad to restore things as they were. And we will do it."

"How long will it take?" Marty asked.

Kaffal said, "It has been done."

Nora said, "How could you possibly load all of the infants into that incubator ship? It would take hours and, surely, you would be seen."

Omborg's phony smile showed itself again. "It will be quite simple. We merely enter the hospital, induce immobility in everyone. Then we create an army of clones, thousands of them. They pick up the infants and load them aboard the shuttle ship and then they are disintegrated again. When our people leave the hospital the people inside are allowed to return to normal but they will have no recollection of what has happened, nor will they know that any children have been stolen. They will not even know why they are in a hospital."

Randy Mapes had listened in silence. But he was angry and obviously trying to control his rage.

"I don't think we will want to help you, Mister Omborg," he said. "If anything, we will oppose you."

Omborg said, "Perhaps I should tell you that we have had to abandon our project. We will not try to remove anyone from this planet. We simply wish to get back to our homeland and we are working on that.

"We invited Miss Nora Corwin to come aboard because we are respectful of her abilities in the field of biology. It was our intention to let Miss Corwin visit and confer with our chief biologist, William Number One. He and his assistants have been responsible for the changes that have taken place on your planet. He discovered the substances that produced a superior type of child in a very short time. Too, he is also the discoverer of the substances that permit women who have just given birth to regain their usual beautiful bodies quickly. It was our hope that Miss Corwin and our William Number One could exchange information and ideas. Naturally, we are quite willing to give you any of our superior secrets. For instance, the control of matter, the ability to become invisible at will, the fine art of telekinesis are some of our more primitive accomplishments. To your people they are miracles. We will be good friends, if you are cooperative and help us to properly calibrate our computer systems."

"Why have you invited me aboard?" Randy Mapes was still angry, still curious. And Omborg was still guileless, charming, politely ingratiating.

"You represent the government of your nation," he said. "If we can persuade you that cooperation from your people is politic and prudent, you will have served your country properly."

"I don't like the threats inherent in what you say."

Omborg sighed. "Perhaps we speak in ways that inflame you but that may be because we are not familiar with your language. I have told you that we have recalled William Number One from his work and there will not be any more babies induced by our methods. The usual procedures are now in force again. We have abandoned our intent to take the infants we want from your planet. Our only need now is to go back to our own planet and that is why we have sought your help. If you and your engineers will help our engineers to make the required corrections we will take off and leave your planet in peace."

Martin sat back in his chair. He was listening, but he found his gaze moving to regard a very pretty blonde girl who seemed to be fascinated by him. She was smiling, slightly, and her eyes seemed to be seeking his at the moment. When Omborg spoke, she stared deep into Martin's eyes and shook her head slightly, almost imperceptibly. Omborg was lying to them. Her eyes seemed to bore deep into his soul and then he heard the things that she did not say.

"They want only to use your machines to correct those we have here and once the corrections have been made we will do as was planned."

He met her stare and the notion that he had seen her before was too strong to shake off. He wondered if he could talk to her in the same way.

"Why do you tell me these things?"

Her brain received his words and answered them. "I am sorry that I did things to threaten you, to hurt you. Thenna has been punished but he is now with Kaspin, the chief of wardens. They are loading infants aboard the space ships and the clones are helping them. You are in great danger. Do be careful."

"Can't others hear us?"

Her smile became wider, warmer. "As long as we lock our eyes and stare deeply, our words become private, inaudible to others. I am Olva. I like you. I would like to help you."

He glanced at Nora and the contact was broken. He was listening to the things that Omborg was saying to Senator Randy Mapes of the United States of America. He didn't like what he was hearing.

"With the powers that we possess we can easily turn this planet into a cinder and destroy the people who live here now. There are many dead planets in space, and their peoples died in much the same fashion that can threaten Earth now. We wish to make corrections to our computers and then we will leave this planet. If we cannot have cooperation then we will simply immobilize all the people we must freeze and then we can home in on the readings that your machines will show us. Once we have made new settings on our computers we will leave here and never return. We mean you and your people no harm. Have I expressed our needs to you clearly?"

Randy Mapes nodded. Martin listened and he nodded, too.

"Then our formal conference is at an end. May we offer you our hospitality? Would you like a tour of our space ship?"

Before they had a chance to answer, a sentinel materialized in front of the triangle. He was a tall man, wearing tight, sheath-like, pants and no shirt. He stood arms folded across a magnificent chest and waited for Omborg to notice him.

Omborg nodded. "You may announce what you have told me," he said.

The sentinel said, "Two men, Orville Corby, who insists that his is the gigantic computer-processing center, and that he has been sent here by a branch of the government, is accompanied by a man named Warren P. Bowman. Bowman insists that he represents the children of the world and they demand an audience. What is your pleasure, Omborg?"

"Bring them aboard," Omborg said. He glanced at the other two supervisors. They nodded slightly, agreeing.

Martin looked at the people seated within the huge triangle. There seemed to be sixty, at least, perhaps more. They were very good-looking specimens of human beings, he supposed, if they were human beings. Perhaps they represented the very cream of the crop where they came from. He supposed that it was only natural, sensible, perhaps would be a better word, to preserve the finest specimens of their breed. There seemed to be an equal number of each sex, they should have been able to multiply on their own planet. If their biologists had been clever enough to develop the three-month gestation period on earth, they could have made it work on their planet, too.

He was still thinking about it when the sentinel came back. He had Orville Corby and Warren P. Bowman with him. They were not at all surprised to find Nora and Randy Mapes with him in the conference room aboard the space ship.

Warren P. Bowman walked up to stand inches away from Omborg. He held his hand out and Omborg disappeared. Warren stared at the empty chair and he turned to look at Martin and the others.

"I only wanted to shake hands," he said. "I didn't mean to alarm him."

Omborg reappeared again. He did not seem to like Warren P. Bowman or Orville Corby.

"What do you men want?" he asked.

Warren P. Bowman stood, tall, resolute, pudgy and bald and beautifully dressed. He fixed Omborg and the others with a truculent stare and his mouth tightened in fierce determination.

"I represent the Institute of Infantile Interests. Anything that concerns the children of our world, concerns me. I have come to tell you that you must not harm the children of this planet. If you have any ideas of kidnapping young people, give it up."

"Are you threatening us?"

Warren P. Bowman stood as straight and tall as he could.

"This is America, the most powerful land on Earth. We have great resources at our command and if we have to ask the military to handle you and your demands, it will not go easy with you, sir."

Omborg was not impressed. "Perhaps it would be wise for us to have an interview with your commander in chief. You call her the president?"

Warren P. Bowman shook his head. Orville Corby

crouched a bit behind him, his thin, angular face filled with dread.

"The President is in Washington," Warren said. "She won't be able to come here, I'm sure."

Omborg twisted slightly in his seat. He touched a button on a small plaque that contained many buttons and a large panel at the other side of the huge room slid aside and exposed a broad expanse of window. They were able to see outside and in moments they were staring at the broad, slender facade of a towering obelisk. It was, unbelievably, unmistakably, the Washington Monument. Martin walked over to get a broader vista and he saw the other buildings of Washington.

The space ship had lifted off of the ground and begun flight without him or any of his party being conscious of it.

"Yes, Mister James," Omborg said. "we are hovering above your establishment and our engineers are adjusting our computers with yours. Hopefully, that will solve our immediate problems."

"Must you run?" Martin asked. "Our people in government and in medicine and the arts, would very much like to meet you and all of your people. We could exchange notes, and, of course, if you want to be charitable, you can teach us a great deal. Why not stay and visit with us for a while?"

A sudden, astonishing clamor arose from the people seated within the triangle. They wanted to stay. They wanted to explore the world that would be new to them.

Omborg held up his hand, palm out. "So be it," he said.

A slender young man with great good looks and dark curly hair entered the chamber. A door slid open to admit him and then slid closed behind him after he passed through it.

Omborg said, "This is our chief engineer. He

designed and installed our computer systems and he had been working on them. How goes it, Pillwick?"

The young man shook his head slowly. "We have made repairs to the machines at the Institute of Applied Logic but they are not constants. The changes in atmosphere affect the delicate balances and it will take some time for us to make all of our required adjustments. Then, when that has been accomplished, we will have to send a shuttle off into space to test the accuracy we have accomplished. Then we can go home."

Martin looked out of the window again and he was surprised to find that they were on the ground again. It seemed that the space ship had settled down on a remote area of Washington's largest airport.

Omborg stood and folded his arms in front of him.

"Gentlemen, I think we can conclude this visit. Mister James, if you will forgive us for the damage that was done to you, we will be grateful. Senator Mapes, if you will notify the people you must, for protocol, we shall be glad to welcome as visitors and friends, your president and other world leaders who may wish to talk with us. Now, gentlemen, you may go back to your labors and leave us to ours."

Warren P. Bowman would not be dismissed. "I want it clearly understood that no babies are going to leave this planet. None whatsoever. I want that clearly understood!"

Omborg waved his hand and the people in the triangle stood and filed out. They stepped onto a moving belt and were carried out of the conference room.

Omborg spoke to Warren P. Bowman smoothly and quietly.

"We are aware of your interest in the very young, and we know, too, that you are sincere in your determination to thwart our efforts to accomplish our

142

purpose. You know that thousands of full-term babies have been born while the infants we are responsible for were born, too. Can you not content yourself with the run-of-the-mill children and let us worry about the others?"

"They are all human beings," Warren said. "And I am determined that no one shall steal them away from here."

Omborg's phony smile appeared. He bowed to each of his visitors in turn.

"We shall see," he said. "We shall see."

Moments later they were outside in the cool air and amid the hordes of curious people who were leaning against the invisible perimeter of the force field.

It seemed that all of Washington was on hand to look at the huge space ship gleaming in the sunshine.

Martin took Nora's hand. "Let's get back to work," he said.

She smiled and nodded. Randy Mapes walked along beside them as they headed for the black limousine that waited. Randy Mapes was eager to talk and as soon as the chauffeur closed the door he began. They sat back and the car began to move out of the airport's V.I.P. parking lot.

"I don't think that we can trust that fellow that we talked to. They are a treacherous crew. And they may be loaded with germs. Brand-new diseases that mankind had never even imagined. What can we do to get rid of them? To conquer them?"

Martin said, "I don't think we have weapons that might intimidate them. They are contemptuous of our most powerful bombs. They just don't fear us in any way."

"What do we do if they try to send a load of infants back to their planet? How do we stop them?"

Martin thought it over slowly before he answered.

"I don't think we can stop them. I can't see how we could."

Randy Mapes sat forward on the edge of the seat.

"I guess we have to turn things over to some other departments now. There's nothing else to do."

He tapped on the glass separating them from the man in front. The chauffeur spoke through the car phone. "Yes, sir?"

"Drop me off at the War Department," Randy Mapes said.

No one in the car objected.

CHAPTER EIGHT

The Institute of Applied Logic was back in business by the time that Nora and Martin James got back to it. David and Lily Trumbull reported that men had come in and worked on the mechanisms that had been ruined and then the machines were humming again, their steady output of information on its way to clients again.

It was late in the day by the time Martin and Nora got the chance to take a break and visit with David and Lily while they pooled information.

They gathered in Martin's office and someone turned on the TV set. Rain was starting to fall, and the drought was broken in England, the Netherlands, and the Northern part of France. The rain was sweeping toward the East and everyone's attention was now riveted on the space ship and Omborg. The heads of state everywhere in the world wanted to call on Omborg and his associates to learn about their advanced scientific studies.

The first overt act happened in Russia, almost predictably. One of the long, cigar-shaped incubator ships surfaced. A veritable army of insignificant people invaded one of the large Russian hospitals and the infants were taken from their cribs and the incubators and loaded aboard the space shuttle ship.

Someone in the Russian military decided to put a stop to the abduction. Several armed tanks were destroyed ramming into a force field that they did not know was in existence. After that, the big cylinder was approached with more caution.

Someone in command panicked when the huge ship began to hum. The area was cleared as quickly as possible and an atomic bomb was detonated right on top of the ship. The theory was that the infants inside would die anyway, but the bomb could make certain that no other infants would be sent off in that particular ship. The explosion was a dull, diminished failure. The energy was absorbed into the force field and the huge space ship took off anyway, only to land at the Washington airport, its precious cargo safe and unfrozen. Nurses from the mother space ship went aboard to take care of the infants.

Omborg told the president of the United States that he and his people intended to dispatch a shuttle ship into outer space in two days. If that ship arrived safely at its destination, others would be dispatched, too.

The president was reduced to a tearful plea, begging Omborg to leave the babies that belonged on earth in their natural environment. It was announced on the TV screen that Omborg refused to commit himself or his people to any agreement. Nora sat beside Martin and watched the TV screen and she turned to him, finally, wondering.

"What do we do now?"

No one answered her. No one seemed to know what would come next. The news cameras spent some time with Warren P. Bowman and he did a lot of blustering on the screen, but it all added up to the same thing. There was no power on earth that could thwart the people from outer space.

After the meeting was over, they went up to the top floor and marveled at the new machines that had been engendered. No one seemed to know quite how the replacements had been accomplished but their accuracy and efficiency were startling.

David said, "I think we've come out ahead. These machines are much more advanced than the ones that were ruined. We have some truly remarkable equipment now."

Nora was worried. "Do you think there is going to be trouble?"

"How can we fight them? Omborg had an interview with some of the big wheels in the government this afternoon and he offered to turn the Washington Monument into dust. He said it was unsightly anyway. The big shots didn't take him up on his offer. I think the way their force field pushed everything out of the way had a sobering effect on a lot of people."

"Maybe that's why they did it," Nora said.

The usual eagerness to be finished with the day and to leave the office seemed to be absent and

Martin finally had to tell everyone to go home. He asked Nora if she would like to have dinner with him and she agreed.

They said good night to the others and went down to the parking lot to get into Nora's car.

She glanced at him as she was maneuvering the car out of the depths of the subterranean garage.

"All right if we go to my place? I can fix us something."

He nodded. They emerged into the street and he was busy looking around him, looking for changes, probably. But there were no changes. Traffic was heavy and people were dashing and plunging in callous disregard of their fellow drivers, and, knowing of the awesome powers that Omborg and his people could exert, Martin wondered if the world was about to undergo a massive change.

Nora flashed him a smile as she found a hole in traffic, zipped into it and out again. He turned the radio on and listened to the newscasters. There was nothing else on.

Omborg was giving out interviews, he was visiting with the important people and he was conducting the sessions from a position of enormous strength. The president, the heads of governments from all nations, went aboard the huge space ship and talked with Omborg and his fellow travelers.

It was announced that the president would speak to the nation at seven that evening.

"I wonder what she can tell us that we don't already know."

He didn't answer her. They parked the car and went inside and Nora fixed drinks for them and they sat down in front of the TV set and smoked cigarettes and tried to relax. It was not easy to do. The television was not at all comforting. The science fictionwriters were at it again, scaring the hell out of the public and, watching, listening, Martin wondered why they were allowed to get on the tube.

Nora finally got to her feet. She finished her drink and stared at the empty glass. "I think I can stand another one," she said. "It's been quite a day. You, too?"

He nodded. She jerked her head at him as she turned to go out to the kitchen. "Come along and keep me company while I fix us something to eat."

He went with her. He stood, his back against the countertop while Nora bustled around, fixing a salad, broiling steaks. They were both startled when the blonde girl, Olva, suddenly materialized a few feet from Marty. She was wearing a short skirt and a white blouse and she looked young and virginal and happy. She reached out to take Marty's hand. She held it for a moment, then she lifted it up, to touch it against her cheek.

"Hello," she said. "I have come to visit with you. I like to visit with you. Will you kiss me?"

Nora was watching, listening, a look of astonishment in her big blue eyes. Martin was sure there was more green in them than usual. Nora was watching him very intently, patently wondering what he was going to do.

"Why would you want me to kiss you?"

She moved close to him, grinding her body against him in a motion that was exceptionally affectionate, and inexpert. She looked up at him and her smile was sparkling, happy.

"I have watched and listened and I find that when people here on Earth like each other they kiss and hold onto each other and I want to try that. I like you very much and I want you to kiss me. Will you?"

Nora's smile seemed a bit strained. "So kiss her," she said. She was holding a head of lettuce in one hand and a small paring knife in the other. He shrugged and pulled the glorious young blonde into his arms. He bent and found the warm, sleek lips with his own and when her lips began to move, and her tongue slipped out to touch his, he shivered as a surge of raw passion swept through him. He pushed the girl away and she stood, panting, gazing at him.

Nora had a startled look on her face. "Well, how about that?" She put the lettuce down and lit a cigarette. She blew smoke towards the ceiling and then turned back to look at Olva.

"I think that's enough of that," she said, firmly.

Olva made a sound that was almost a giggle. "Oh, I'm sorry," she said. "It was so nice. I would like to try it again."

Martin smiled. "I don't think we'd better."

Olva made a slight movement with her hand and Nora became a statue. She twisted to smile up at him. "Now she will not know. Kiss me, please. I like it when we kiss."

He kissed her, knowing that it was more a clinical bit of business than anything else. Olva's mouth was pressed tightly to his own and her lips crawled and worked against him with an expertise that was quite amazing. She stepped back, finally, and her eyes held a look of startled wonder. Her head was tilted to one side as she looked up at him.

"I have heard about love, too," she said. "Do you love the girl, Nora?"

He nodded. "Yes, I do. I love her very much."

"Why don't you marry?"

He looked at Nora, lovely and young and frozen in a posture of suspended animation and he went close to her, he reached out to touch her immobilized body. He kissed her and it was like kissing a girl who had fallen asleep.

"Nora doesn't want to get married," he said.

Olva's smile twinkled. "She may change her mind now," she said. She moved back into his embrace and her mouth sought his. Her kiss was ardent, moist, seeking, a thing of great joy to her, obviously.

150

When she finally let him go, he found that Nora was restored to her usual self. She was gazing at him with a brand-new look in her eyes.

"I must go," Olva said. "We are not allowed to roam at will."

A moment later, he and Nora were alone again.

"I wanted to talk to her," he said. "There are so many questions I wanted answers for."

Waspishly, Nora said, "She got answers to her questions."

He reached for Nora and kissed her. She tried to wriggle out of his embrace but she did not fight him as hard as usual. After a moment of struggling, she relaxed against him and their kiss became warm and sweet and she began to tremble in his arms. When he let her go, she stared at him and he could see the tears shimmering in her eyes.

"I do love you, you know," he said.

Her face wore a woebegone look. "I love you, too. But, that is as far as I want to go at the moment."

He kissed her again. "It's a start," he said.

They talked about Olva and her people and their remarkable powers to appear and disappear and he pointed out that mankind was very close to a breakthrough in learning how to handle matter.

They continued talking through dinner. Nora was very worried about the future of the world as she knew it.

"Surely they must know that they need only to decide that they want to inhabit and rule this planet and all of their highly touted trips back home would be totally unnecessary. They may decide to take over the planet Earth. Then what?"

He shook his head, slowly, thinking about what she had said. "I think the homing instinct is strong in them. They want to go home to the kind of life they have always known."

"What happens when they try to send thousands,

maybe millions, of infants back to their homeland?"

"I don't know," he said. "I frankly don't know."

She leaned back in her chair and jeered at him. "The great Martin James without an answer."

He grinned. He took a sip of his coffee and put the cup down. "You know me; without my computers, I'm nothing."

They watched the newscast until it was very late and then he called a taxi. He promised Nora that he would see her early in the morning and when they kissed good night he found a new and delightful warmth in her kiss.

He found Randy Mapes waiting for him at the office the next morning. The senator was worn and tired. He had been up all night, talking with the military people and he admitted that he had wasted his time. He sat down in front of Martin's desk and the receptionist brought coffee. Nora came in to join them followed by David and Lily.

"I just don't know what we can do about the situation," Randy Mapes said. "We can't stop them, and we can't let them freeze thousands of infants and take them from us, either."

David plucked his glasses out of his shirt pocket and started to put them on. Lily reached out and stopped him. She put his glasses back into his pocket. "It is not a time for speeches, David," she said, firmly. He nodded absently and sat back in silence.

Lily said, "It is such a shame they have to have infants. If they would only put an ad in the paper they would get millions of people who would love to go off and repopulate their planet. If I didn't have David and my nice job, I'd want to go myself."

A sudden silence developed in the office and Martin James stared at Randy Mapes. Lily slid out to the edge of the seat and looked around at them. "I said something important?"

"You may have given us the solution to our problem," Martin said. "We'll have to see."

David said, "Out of the mouths of infants and idiots come words of wisdom."

Lily twisted to kiss his cheek. "You don't know which I am, dear," she said. "Isn't that nice."

Randy Mapes went to the videophone. He began making calls, trying to arrange an audience with Omborg and his people. No one seemed to know how to go about it.

"I'll try something," Martin said. He tried to concentrate upon the image of Omborg. He spoke his thought aloud. "I wish to see you, Omborg. I wish to talk with you."

Omborg materialized before them in seconds. He was genial, smiling, glad to see them again. He seemed to feel that he was among friends.

"What do you wish to talk about?" He sat down in a vacant chair. Martin got to the point right away.

"Must you send infants back to your planet?"

Omborg stared at him, not at all sure of what was in Martin's mind. And that was unusual for Omborg.

"Our world and its people will not let you take its infants from our land without trying to stop you. That, of course, means an unnecessary loss of life. Now, why can't you take adults? Grown-up people?"

Omborg stared at him. "Grown-up people would go?"

Martin said, "If you advertise for volunteers, thousands of people will show up, begging for the chance to go to a new world. Your people can examine them and take the fittest. And leave us our babies. Would you consider that?"

Omborg stood up. He looked at Randy Mapes and he seemed to exude a new and warmer friendliness toward them.

"This is something we had not considered. We

thought of sending infants to our planet because they would be malleable and easy to train to our ways. But grown people who really wanted to become pioneers in a new world might be even better. You really think Earth people would want to go?"

Randy Mapes nodded. "Thousands will want to go. Millions, perhaps. Why not try it?"

Omborg said, "I must submit this idea to my council. I will let you know what they decide."

He disappeared again.

When they were about ready to end their session, Lily arose and faced them with an impish smile. She huffed on her nails and rubbed them briskly against her blouse.

"I hope you guys recognize a little ol' genius when you run into one. *I* may have come up with the answer."

David grabbed her and kissed her. "We'll hope," he said.

Randy Mapes said he had to go to his office.

"We can keep up to date by just watching the newscasts.

Randy Mapes left and Nora went off to her office and David and Lily went to their labs. Martin sat behind his desk for a time, wondering if they had finally solved the insoluble problem.

He switched on the TV set and watched it. And there was much to watch. He moved from station to station. He found Amy Driscoll on one channel. She was being interviewed by a famous newsman and from what they were saying, Martin could put together a strange story.

Three men in an expensive limousine were involved in a minor automobile accident and the police found more than a million dollars in cash in two suitcases in the limousine. The men were taken to jail and, under questioning, revealed that the money had been given to them by Warren P. Bowman.

The head of the Institute for Infantile Interests was in jail and his entire organization was being investigated.

The newscaster seemed to regard Warren P. Bowman as the world's worst thief and mountebank.

"The world knows that you have defended some really unpopular cases," the man said, "but, do you feel that you really want to defend Warren P. Bowman? I mean, now that the whole world knows what he has been doing?"

Amy Driscoll wore the look that Joan of Arc must have worn as she approached the stake.

"I have always been very fond of Warren P. Bowman," Amy said, rather stiffly. "I will defend him, of course."

The newsman seemed to be surprised. "He's the worst kind of hypocrite," he said. "Bowman's been spreading the story that he solicits donations from the people he can control for the sick and the forlorn children of the world. Actually he has a gang of henchmen that launder the money for him and then put it in a private, numbered account. Now we know all about him. How can you defend that kind of a man?"

Amy looked unhappy. "I'm afraid that I am in love with that kind of a man. And I will try to help him. Perhaps I can change him."

The newsman looked ill. His attitude seemed to suggest that a pretty girl like Amy could find better things to do.

Amy said, "Like you and everyone else, I suppose, I didn't know that he was doing these things. But, I know it now."

"The whole world knows it now." he said.

The picture shifted and other news crowded Warren P. Bowman's beleaguered attorney off the screen.

Kaffal, representing the space people, was interviewed and he had much to say.

"We are sending the shipload of infants that were taken from the Russian hospitals back to their proper environment. We have been told that many Earth people might like to visit our planet and help us to develop a new civilization. We will be glad to talk with any such volunteers. Those whose health and moral character will recommend them as future citizens of Rombella may apply at our space ship.

"It has been decided that we will have no need to send infants into space if we can interest adults. Frankly, we would rather have adults."

Martin, watching, heard a sound behind him. Lily had walked in. She was quite proud of herself. She held up her hands and her fingers were crossed.

"I hope there really are many people on earth who will want to try life on a new planet."

Martin smiled. "I'm sure that there are."

Kaffal came to see him shortly after lunch. He asked if technicians from the space ship could use Martin's facilities to check their own readings. They wanted to triangulate, using the institute's equipment and then the equipment aboard the three big jets in other parts of the world.

Kaffal stood in Martin's office and he was suddenly diffident.

"We became aware that there were many crippled infants since we left the salt mine. Several of our physicians are visiting the children's hospital and we can promise that there will be no crippled or sick children by nightfall. Several of our biologists and bacteriologists are upstairs, feeding as much of

156

our medical knowledge and expertise into your banks as possible."

Martin was amazed.

Kaffal smiled. "We hope that your people will think kindly of us, no matter what we must do."

Kaffal disappeared then. Martin lit a cigarette and then walked over to the window wall. He gazed out at the gleaming white bulk of the space ship parked some distance away.

He noticed that there were huge crowds gathering at the edges of the roped-off spaces. He supposed that they were the curious. More and more people seemed to be arriving even as he watched.

Nora came to meet him for lunch. She went to the window, and looked out at the growing crowd.

She said, "I can't imagine why the military would allow such a large mob to gather. That could mean trouble."

David and Lily arrived to join them for lunch. David was up to date with the latest news and explained the crowd.

"Those are people who want to go to Rombella. The government is setting up recruiting stations everywhere. They are also using schools and military recruiting stations. It is astonishing how many people still possess the pioneering spirit."

They stopped watching the crowds and went down to the garage. As they were about to get into Nora's car, Olva appeared. She was standing beside Martin, smiling up at him.

"Kaffal is very grateful to you," she said. "We will be able to select many new citizens from the masses now coming to us. Kaffal asked me to convey his thanks."

"What ever happened to Omborg?" Nora said. "I thought he was number one man."

Olva said, "Omborg has been banished into outer space in one of the cocoons. He would not give up the babies. He would not cooperate with Earth people. Kaffal would like it if we can all be friends."

Nora moved close to Olva. "We can be friends, but no more kissing. Absolutely none. No more of that."

Olva's pretty face wore a baffled look. "Oh, I am sorry. I liked that. I really did."

Nora slipped her hand into Martin's. "I like it, too," she said, firmly. "I'll do all of it from now on."

Olva moved her hand and Nora became immobile. Martin glanced at David and Lily. They were frozen, too.

Olva stepped so close that she was touching him. She lifted her mouth up and then she was kissing him, warmly, sweetly, passionately. He shivered as he realized that he liked the lovely young girl.

She moved away from him and her eyes were filled with sadness. "We will go home very soon now," she said, "but we will come back to Earth again and again. I will see you in the future. I promise. While I am away, will you think of me kindly? Will you?"

"I will always remember you. I will always like you."

She smiled, happily. She kissed him once more and then she faded away.

Nora put her hand into his.

"Let's eat, shall we?"

He nodded. He got the door open and Lily and David got in. He sat down beside Nora. She drove out of the garage into the brilliant sunshine of the day and he was filled with a new kind of happiness. He would go on working with his friends and associates and maybe Nora would listen to reason about love and marriage and the good life.

He knew that he would always remember Olva. And he would always like her.

He would like her very much.

Always.